The Seven Days of Christmas

Book 1 of "Days of…" Series

By: Sharon D. Tweet

Enjoy the journey!
Sharon D. Tweet

Cover photo by Sharon D. Tweet
Cover design by Tweets Unlimited
Author photo by Julie Bannister, Even When Photography

The Seven Days of Christmas
Book 1 of "Days of..." Series
by Sharon D. Tweet
ISBN-13: 978-1539774440
ISBN-10: 1539774449

This book is a work of fiction. Names, characters, places, and incidents are the product of the author's imagination and are used factiously. Any resemblance to actual events, locales or persons, living or dead, is coincidental.

Dear Reader, This book is dedicated to you. May you be inspired to love passionately, live purposefully, and share God's word boldly.

ACKNOWLEDGEMENT:

What a fun journey this has been – diving into the world of publishing. Independent publishing, no less. I certainly didn't see this coming for me. But, God has a way of bringing new adventures into our lives; adventures we'd never dream of for ourselves. And that is exactly what this process has been, an adventure. Like all good adventures, this has filled me with excitement, doubt, fear, insecurity, confidence, the opportunity to learn new things, and a continued faith and trust in the Lord and His direction. And, like all good adventures, I've been blessed to experience it with others along the way.

Michelle Isenhoff, Tracy Groot, and Susie Finkbeiner you each encouraged me, welcomed me, and made me feel at ease at my very first venture into the world of publishing at my very first writer's conference. Each of you has played a roll in my journey, and I am thankful for the way God placed you in my path.

Kim Luke you have inspired me to follow this crazy journey of self-publishing and stay the course through the hard work. Your time, your encouragement, and the friendship you showed me have meant so much.

Sarah, what a gift you gave me reading through my story for the first time as my first unofficial editor – even though you don't like reading Christian fiction romance. I have been blessed by you in so many ways. And Nancy, thank you for giving me insight and editing advice as I drew closer to publishing; I can't tell you how much you helped and encouraged me.

Janelle, I am thrilled you liked my story. And I love that you didn't think you would like it, but you read it, hesitantly, anyway, because you're my friend. I'm pleased and humbled that I was able to surprise you.

Thadd, Isaiah and Elijah, I'm so beyond thankful that you are my family. I love you more than words can express. Thank you for being my support. Thadd, thank you for never making me feel like this was a silly pipe dream, but always encouraging me to just do it. Elijah, thank you for being so willing to jump in and offer help and encouragement along the way.

CHAPTER 1

She'd slept in that morning. Snuggled under a pile of blankets, she stayed warm and cozy while quiet Christmas jazz music played on her iPod docking station; the smooth soulful rhythm had become a soothing balm to her tender emotions. As the sleepy fog cleared from her mind and her eyes began to focus, she pushed back the thick layer of covers, let her legs fall off the side of the bed and lifted her tired and weary body, coaxing it into following suit.

It was the week before Christmas. The snow outside was more than two feet deep covering the houses and yards and trees in a shimmering coverlet. Everything shone brightly in the late morning winter sun looking clean and refreshed. Christmas lights and festive decorations adorned most of the houses up and down the block. Every year, her home had been lit up and decorated, filling her home and her heart with all the joy and cheer of the holiday season. Every year, that is, except that one.

Traditionally the yard nativity her father built years

ago claimed a large portion of the front lawn. Claiming the spot that year, tucked beneath a blue tarp, skids were piled with lumber, boxes of tile and other construction supplies. The spacious corner in the living room that usually displayed a beautifully decorated Christmas tree lighting up the room with cheer, instead contained stacks of boxes and a make-shift temporary kitchen. In lieu of hanging swags of garland and cinnamon pine cones and bows, plastic tarps and extension cords were strung from scattered hooks. The fragrances of Christmas that had always tantalized and permeated her home – sugar cookies cooling on the counter, apple cider simmering in the crock pot, and pumpkin nut bread baking in the oven –were replaced by the powerful scent of fresh cut wood, paint and stain.

She and her brother had undertaken the monumental task of remodeling their home's kitchen over the summer. Summer, however, quickly transitioned into autumn which had eventually become winter. As a result of all the construction and the displaced kitchen, there really was not space to decorate for Christmas. Much of their free time had been spent working on the project. And, of course, each had a career that required time and attention leaving little time or focus to think about or add anything else. Or, maybe those were just excuses to cover over the pain of sadness and loss they felt that holiday season. Consequently, the ability to summon the Christmas Spirit had been elusive. And there it was, a week before Christmas.

She had just finished brushing her teeth when she heard her brother greet someone at the front door. From the sound of the greeting, it could only be one person. A smile spread across her face. *He's here,* she thought, filled with an unexpected flutter. She shook off the feeling as she exited the bathroom to descend the stairs. As she neared the bottom she could see two men engulfed in a brotherly embrace. The front door was wide open, allowing the cold winter air to pour in. Someone stood slightly back hovering in the shadow of the doorway. Her eyes, however, focused solely on him, never registering the other person at the door or what he carried in his hands.

"Ah, there she is. Good morning, Sunshine." Looking up over Jackson's shoulder, Rick smiled. Both men parted and released from their greeting before Rick stepped to the side to envelope Caroline in a full bear hug.

"Good morning, Ricky. I didn't think we'd see you until tonight." Caroline wrapped her arms around him and hugged him tight. She was so glad to see him.

Jackson and Rick met their junior year of college when Rick filled the need for a fourth roommate at Jackson's apartment. The two hit it off and had been best friends since. After Rick came home with Jackson for Thanksgiving and

Christmas breaks that year, he seemed to fit so perfectly within the family that he became just that - a new member of the family. Caroline was sixteen years old and affectionately dubbed him 'Ricky'; that was fourteen years ago.

Rick pulled back from their embrace. He looked directly at Caroline with a hint of a smile. "Oh, I just wanted to bring a little something by for you guys. I decided the house could use a little Christmas cheer." Resting his index finger under her chin, tenderly he added, "And I thought maybe you could, too." He stepped back and swept his hand in the direction of the young man who'd entered behind him.

Jackson had already let him in the house, closed the door and was leading him toward the living room. Rick explained, "That's Caleb Puchansky, the new intern I was telling you about."

Caroline followed Rick's gaze toward Jackson and Caleb as they wound their way through the maze of furniture and boxes in the living room. They chatted amiably. Jackson always had an easy time putting new people at ease and making anyone feel like an old friend. Although Caroline also knew that they had already met. Caleb carried a small table top Christmas tree, complete with burlap root ball, tiny lights and cute little package and bow ornaments. Jackson cleared off a space on one of the TV trays. Caleb placed the little tree on the stand while Jackson fumbled around with an extension cord. Once he found an empty space, he plugged in the festive little tree.

While Caroline stood and stared, Rick watched her reaction. Caroline's eyes began to well with tears.

"Oh, come on, Sunshine, it was supposed to make you smile, not cry." Rick bridged the small gap between them and wrapped her in a playful embrace. "Looks like I'll just have to wrestle you into some laughter."

Caroline held on tight so as not to fall over. Just as quickly as the tears threatened to fall, they faded away and she giggled into his chest. "Please, no, Ricky! I'm not dressed for wrestling!"

With his arms securely around her waist, he leaned out just far enough to look down and notice her shorts and tank top pajama set underneath her bulky fleece robe. Her fuzzy purple slippers skated along the floor. Rick took in a breath and he felt a peace wash over him as he realized, *This is it, this is my moment.*

With a glint in his eye Rick asked her, "Are you dressed for hugging?"

She closed her eyes and held him tight; her arms wrapped around his head. She whispered in his ear, "Yes, I think I'm dressed for hugging. Thank you, Ricky."

* * * * *

Rick had always treated Caroline with the utmost respect. Her brother's friendship meant the world to him and it always came first. Jackson had a rule for his friends – his sister was off limits. She was not to be flirted with, toyed with or messed around with. Before he even got in the car to drive home with Jackson that very first Thanksgiving, Jackson had expressed his unyielding rule. Break the rule, lose the friendship; it was that simple. Rick couldn't argue with a big brother who showed such love and protection for his little sister, and he really respected Jackson for being so upfront. They had built their own brotherly bond over the first few months of knowing each other and with no family of his own, Rick valued the friendship immensely.

When Rick met Caroline for the first time it was a real treat for Rick. There was a pretty, perky, happy, smiling sixteen year old that looked up at him with big, innocent emerald green eyes. It would have taken but a moment to ease into a discreet flirtation that he could string out over distance and time. If he played his cards right he could enjoy the benefits of her innocent affection when visiting with the family on holiday while still maintaining his friendship with Jackson.

With Caroline's hand in his at their initial introduction and Jackson's watchful gaze on him over her shoulder, he had a split second to make his choice. "Your little sister's like a ball of sunshine, Jackson. Cute." And he shook her hand and gave her a playful, brotherly punch on her shoulder. That's all it took. It was the kiss of death to any hope of romance between the two. She'd rolled her eyes, let out a huff and turned to play with the family dog while, unbeknownst to Caroline, Jackson smiled and gave a slight approving nod to Rick. That was how their friendship began, and that was where Caroline got her nickname, Sunshine. It stuck, and he'd called her that ever since.

* * * * *

Ricky had always been safe. Caroline knew about Jackson's rule. It irked her most of the time growing up, but she always knew she was safe from unwanted advances, especially when some of Jackson's friends had been less than savory characters. She always knew Jackson had her back. Ricky had made his choice a long time ago – his friendship with Jackson was the most important friendship he had and he would not do anything to jeopardize it. He'd become like another big brother to Caroline. He was safe. He was a good confidant and, over the years, he had become one of, if not *the*, best friend she'd ever had, next to the Lord and her brother.

Caroline had watched with sadness Rick's womanizing and drinking. She had watched, with pride, his hard work as he completed his internship and his master's program. She had also watched, with a joy and love so deep it made her ache *and* want to shout aloud with glee, as both he and Jackson discovered for themselves six years ago her first love, Jesus Christ. Since that time, the three of them had spent countless hours in Bible study, prayer and discussion. The bond they shared was unlike anything she could possibly describe.

* * * * *

For a moment Rick and Caroline swayed in big dips, engulfed in their big bear hug, at the foot of the stairs. Slowly, their surroundings began to blur, and the voices in the living room became hushed and faded. Faint music wafted down the stairs from Caroline's room and their grand swaying dips eased into a slow, intimate dance. Their big bear hug relaxed into a gentle, almost sensual, embrace. Safety began to slip into security.

Caroline could feel the gentleness of his touch on the small of her back as he pulled her closer; the fierce pounding of his heart against his chest. Her arms floated across his shoulders in a motion so soft and tender, she questioned whether the sparks she felt were real or imaginary. Her fingers entwined his thick, wavy dark hair at the base of his neck. As her breath became short and shallow, a tingle of energy rushed up her spine and through every part of her body. Nestled close to her ear she felt the warmth of his breath and heard the quiet, hope-filled words, "Have dinner with me tonight, Caroline."

Her fingers still caressed his hair and neck as she leaned out only far enough to see the look in his chocolate brown eyes. She had caught him looking at her like that more and more over the past several months. It always made her breathless, as it did in that moment. Each time before she quickly looked away, unsure of what she saw, or what she felt. She would never do anything to upset the relationship she shared with both Rick and her brother, or their friendship.

That time Caroline looked fully into his face. There was no mistaking what she saw. Brotherly affection had moved out and been replaced with desire, heartfelt hope, adoration and, what?

"I thought we already were; the three of us." There was questioning concern in her tone and her eyes, but she remained entwined in his arms.

Although his hands held her in the solid and secure embrace of a strong and confident man, his voice betrayed the vulnerability of a teenager as he said, "I've spoken with

Jackson." Awkwardly he continued, "and he's, well, he's given his permission."

In a heartbeat the full ramifications of Rick's statement flooded her thoughts. She hadn't been losing her mind; the feelings she was struggling with, he was, too. The fluctuations in looks and tone of voice; all those mixed signals and confusing feelings; the sparks of electricity at the touch of his hand; it wasn't just her imagination. And he had spoken with Jackson.

All the conversations about relationships she and Jackson had had lately made a new kind of sense. She wondered how long he and Jackson had been talking. *Is this real? Ricky wouldn't play around like this. Would he? No. This must be real.*

Rick continued to watch her features. *Wish I knew what she was thinking.* "Caroline?" There was hesitation in his voice as his assurance waivered and he felt a twinge of doubt. "Have I… misread things?"

"I, I don't know what to say." Caroline lowered her eyes as her hands slid down the front of his torso. Through his button down shirt she could feel the toned form of his body as she moved her hands. Shrouded in the opening of his long winter coat, she rested her hands at his waist. Mixed with excitement and anticipation, her fears, doubts and insecurities began to cloud her mind.

He tilted his head down to catch her gaze and smiled. His confidence returned. He kept one hand around her waist, lifted his other hand and slid it along her neck, under her jaw. His thumb caressed the side of her cheek sending a wave of heat and electricity through each of them. He looked deep into her emerald green eyes and said, “Say yes.”

She sighed, closed her eyes, leaned her head into his hand and, with the sweetest hint of a smile, said, “Yes.”

With a sense of relief and gratitude, he leaned down and brushed a soft kiss on her forehead. They stood for another moment, foreheads touching, each with their eyes closed; silently they drank in the moment before the rest of the world returned to focus.

“Alright, Rick,” Jackson bellowed through the house, “have you succeeded in cheering up my melancholy sister yet? You’d think she was a teenager on school holiday, deprived of any social contact with her peers, as late as she slept this morning.” He and Caleb weaved their way back through the maze of the living room.

Each man carried a chocolate donut and coffee in a paper travel cup. Apparently Jackson had taken Caleb into the kitchen to show off their work. The coffee maker was one of the few appliances set up in their makeshift kitchen, and the donut indicated that Jackson had been out earlier to pick up a treat.

Rick and Caroline parted and looked at Jackson. "I think we're all good here," said Rick with an almost indiscernible nod toward Jackson. Turning all attention away from the two of them, he said, "Hey that looks good. Where's mine?" and he threw a dejected look at Caleb.

A little panicked, Caleb stammered, "Um, oh, sorry, sir. If you'd like," he began turning back toward the living room, "I can go get you…"

Rick and Jackson both started to laugh. Swiping Rick with the belt of her robe, Caroline reprimanded both men. "Oh, stop it, both of you. Don't pick on him. Caleb, pay them no mind. Rick is a big boy. If he wants coffee, he knows where to get it. You're his intern, not his errand boy." She held out her hand in greeting. "Sorry for the attire; I don't usually greet guests in my robe. Hi, I'm Caroline Atherton."

Caleb juggled his coffee to the hand with his donut as he looked at her with a sense of relief and a lopsided grin. He looked to be about twenty years old and six feet tall, appearing to split the height difference between Jackson and Rick. Clean cut and nice looking, his dark hair was fashionably slicked over with a side part. His crystal blue eyes were shockingly clear and bright. A simple suit with a conservative tie gave him a sharp, polished appearance. Although he displayed a quietly confident air, he was also a little green and eager to please the big boss man.

After Rick received his Master of Architecture degree, he took a job with a large architectural firm in the city. There he eagerly accepted every opportunity to work on a variety of different projects, which allowed him to hone his skills and network to build a rather impressive list of contacts. He also inserted himself into as many aspects of the business as he could; his desire to learn all the ins and outs of the business side of an architectural firm propelled him.

About four years ago, Rick took a leap of faith and struck out on his own. After a rocky first year some of those earlier contacts had begun to bear fruit and his business started to flourish. Now, he housed two full time architects, an office manager, and an assistant. His talent, solid work ethic and attention to detail had established him with an estimable reputation. As his business continued to grow he made the decision, for the second year in a row, to hire an intern from his alma mater.

Caleb had just started with Rick's firm the first week of December and was having a little trouble deciphering his new boss's sense of humor. Thankful for the intervention, he took Caroline's outstretched hand. "So, you're the illustrious Miss Atherton. It's so nice to finally meet you."

Caroline suppressed a giggle and said, "Illustrious? Oooh, I like that." She flashed him a smile and said, "Let me guess – a double minor in English?"

A little embarrassed, Caleb just nodded.

Caroline released Caleb's hand and turned toward Rick before continuing. "Treat this one nice, Ricky, he just might help refine you a little bit, bring a little sophistication to your humble establishment." With more than a little affection and a lot of sassy, she straightened Rick's tie and stuck out her tongue at him.

Rick threw his head back and his arms up. "Oh, that's it. I am not sticking around for any more of this abuse. I bring you a lovely little tree for Christmas and this is the thanks I get. Oh, the abuse!" Although said with a straight face, there was no mistaking the gleam in his eyes as he delivered his brief outburst with dramatic flair. "Mr. Puchansky, I think it's time for us to take our leave." Hand over his chest, head held high, he turned to open the front door.

With a wide grin on his face, Caleb responded, "Yes, sir, Mr. Stratford, sir." It was evident he'd caught on quickly to that little ruse.

Both men exited the house and stoically marched to the deep blue Jeep Liberty parked at the curb. Jackson stepped into the home's threshold and called out, "Hey, good luck on that presentation today, brother."

Rick glanced up over the top of the vehicle, smiled, and gave a brief salute to Jackson before he threw a quick wink at Caroline. He ducked into his Jeep and the two were off.

Closing the door, Jackson turned to Caroline, draped his arm over her shoulders and the two turned toward the living room. "Well, little sister, we have ourselves a bon-a-fide Christmas tree. Do you feel better?"

Staring at the tiny sparkle coming from deep within the room, she chuckled. "Actually, I do a little. It was awfully thoughtful of Ricky to do that."

"Yea, it really was," Jackson said as he looked at his sister. "But, he knows how hard this time has been; he just wants to make it a little easier for you." He looked back at the living room and continued. "And, hey, sis, I really am sorry this," he grandly swept his arm to encompass the house, "is taking so long and it's adding to the difficulty of the holidays for you. It wasn't supposed to be this way."

The genuine concern in her brother's tone touched her heart. She sighed a heavy sigh. "None of this was supposed to be this way. And this," she pointed at the house, "isn't your fault; you have nothing to apologize for. I'm the one who should be apologizing. I know I've been sullen and melancholy, and I'm truly sorry. If the holidays have felt ruined, it's my own fault. I know holiday spirit isn't about decorations and trimmings – it's about remembering Jesus' birth and spending time with and appreciating the special people in our lives."

She sighed again and continued. "With our numbers a little smaller this year, it's making me, well, it's making me sad and gloomy. But I can't begin to tell you how much I appreciate you in my life, you and Ricky, both. Will you forgive me?"

He squeezed her shoulder and kissed her on the side of the head. "Forgiveness given, sis, but nothing to forgive. It's been hard for me, too, and Rick. We'll get through this together, just like we have been; the good, the bad and the melancholy."

The deep resonate chime of the antique grandfather clock in the corner of the foyer was Jackson's cue. "Ten o'clock, time for me to scat. I've got that meeting with all the rec. center coaches before lunch. Wish me luck. I'm really excited about the proposals for next year."

* * * * *

Jackson had always been good at sports - not just one in particular, but most of them. He was what his parents referred to as a natural athlete. And Jackson liked to play. He liked the rules. He liked the challenge. He liked the competition, the camaraderie of the team and the physical fitness required to perform. And he loved that throughout the seasons the sports changed. Midway through high school he began to toss around the idea that he should focus on one sport and pursue something with a future in the professional arena. But, since he hated to limit his involvement, he decided to play it by ear; if scouts sought him out in a particular season, he would see what came of it. Until such time, he'd chosen to play and grow and learn – and have fun.

One day during an intense rivalry hockey game, Jackson had the misfortune of landing at the center of a series of destructive circumstances. His skate stuck in a groove in the ice at the same moment he turned to receive a pass while his opponent had his sights set on a check into the boards. The combination resulted in a serious compound fracture of his right tibia and a torn MCL in his knee. Although he recovered beautifully from his injuries, after months of intense physical therapy, he would never play on a professional level. Jackson had to re-evaluate his future.

Thankfully, Jackson also held good grades. Good enough to earn a scholarship to his school of choice where he pursued a BA in Sport's Management. That choice led him to his employment by the city as their Park & Recreation Activities Director. Like everything else he put his effort into, he excelled at his job. He designed programs and camps, arranged tournaments, lined up staff and coach's training seminars; he even helped out with coaching when he could. He had found a passion for fostering a love of sports, teamwork and physical fitness in the community.

* * * * *

Jackson grabbed his coat from the rack in the foyer and put on his stocking cap. He bent down to pick up his laptop case and stopped to look at his sister. "Oh, by the way, what's the plan for dinner tonight?"

For a brief moment Caroline internally panicked. *What if he gets upset?* She immediately squashed that thought. *No, they've talked about this. He'll be fine. Right? Here goes...* "Yea, about dinner, um, actually, uh, Ricky has asked me… out… to dinner tonight." She looked him square in the face, held her breath, and waited.

He didn't hesitate for a second before a knowing smile spread across his face. "Finally! I was beginning to wonder if he was ever going to follow through. It must've been your purple fuzzy slippers that got him this morning."

Caroline breathed a sigh of relief. She knew what Ricky had said, but she could not breathe easy until she had heard it for herself. She sought once more for the confirmation of his approval. Her eyes and tone full of questions, she asked, "You're really okay with this?"

Jackson stepped close to his sister and hugged her.

Looking down into her questioning eyes he smiled and asked, “Do you want to go out to dinner with him?”

She lowered her gaze, smiled shyly and softly bit the inside of her cheek. She nodded her head before returning her gaze to her brother.

“Well okay, then,” Jackson said with kind confirmation. “And, yes, I’m totally okay with this.” He gave her shoulder a squeeze of encouragement. “Have fun tonight. And plan on getting up early tomorrow, like seven o’clock early, to have breakfast with me. I’ll make your favorite omelet and we can chat. K?” He was headed toward the front door.

Caroline felt all of her brother’s encouragement clear away any cloud of concern or doubt she had. She smiled and said, “Thanks, Jackson. And okay, it’s a date. Good luck today.”

CHAPTER 2

Alone in her house, Caroline stood in front of the little table top Christmas tree and smiled. It was such a thoughtful gesture. And it really did lift her spirits. Or was it the slow dance she'd shared with Ricky at the bottom of the stairs that made the difference? *But we dance together all the time,* she thought. She grinned as she reveled in the memory of his touch. *But not like that. That was different.*

Or was it the fact that she had a genuine date with Ricky later that night that caused such a drastic shift in her focus? "Oh, what does it matter? I feel festive and it feels good!" she said aloud. She smiled at the tree, pulled off the instruction tag and waltzed over to the makeshift kitchen to make some coffee and grab a donut.

She turned her favorite chair so she could gaze at the little tree while she savored her coffee. Coffee never tasted quite as good in a paper cup as it did in a real mug, but she would pretend, just like she had been doing for the past five months. She wrapped her fingers around the cup and allowed the warmth to radiate through her fingers and spread up her arms. Closing her eyes, she leaned her head back against the chair and once again allowed herself to relive every moment of her slow dance with Ricky just a short time ago.

She lingered in her mind's eye at every movement, every touch and every implication. In the moment she had said yes to dinner, she'd made the same type of choice Ricky made all those years ago. That was not a date she would take lightly. But, then again, Caroline never had dated lightly.

Caroline had decided long ago to pursue a more old-fashioned notion of courtship rather than the common practice of dating. Her commitment to chastity and purity was unusual, even within the church. But, she chose to set her values, her expectations and her standards by the guidelines she found in God's word and the convictions she felt from Him. That was not necessarily a popular approach in the current day and age, even among her peers. As she got older it became even more difficult.

She didn't particularly like how much her choices set her apart from others, but she refused to apologize for how she felt. She hoped she never came off as judging of others who made different choices, but she was afraid her convictions were, well, convicting. Too often it seemed to be an issue that put a strain on friendships.

Her roommate from college and the ladies from her

singles small group at church seemed to follow pretty closely to the same commitment. That served as a bond between them. It also allowed them to be a source of encouragement for each other.

As far as men were concerned, Caroline trusted that God had given her such a commitment for a reason and if He had a special guy picked out for her, then he would not think she was weird because of her beliefs or her approach.

As a result, Caroline had only pursued two serious relationships. The first was in her second year of college. The young man was a fellow student in the Biblical Studies department. Although he proved to be an excellent study partner and someone with whom she could hash out difficult scriptural concepts, he turned out to be a little too legalistic in his approach to walking out his faith within the confines of a romantic relationship. They mutually agreed to "just be friends".

The second relationship she pursued was with a man she'd met while photographing a beautiful old winery for their new brochures. His name was Thom. Caroline and Thom were very compatible; each had a strong commitment to the Lord and desired to pursue Him first. They were in complete agreement about their cautious and conservative approach to a romantic relationship. It was all very proper.

Things had moved along so nicely with Thom that

Caroline contemplated whether or not he was "the one". One night, on his way home after a lovely evening at the theatre, Thom was killed in a tragic automobile accident. Caroline was left feeling numb. She doubted if she would ever find the kind of love and devotion she so desired.

As she sat there in her chair, mesmerized by the twinkle of lights from the little tree, Caroline began to reflect on the past year or so with Ricky. She tried to scrutinize all the details. *When was it, exactly, that my feelings began to change?* she pondered. So often she would push away any inkling of a romantic feeling or thought of him because he was Ricky, Jackson's best friend, her safe friend. That just was not possible.

Any possibility of romance with Ricky also was not realistic. Ricky had led a much more wild life before he surrendered his life to the Lord six years ago. What would he want with a naive, innocent girl like her? *He'd never want to get serious with a girl like me,* she thought over and over. And yet, that was exactly what she was looking at – getting serious with Ricky.

For the first time, Caroline let all the looks, all the electric touches and all the winks focus in her mind. She recalled all the hugs that lasted just a little longer than they used to, and all the times he had held open her door and escorted her through with his hand on the small of her back.

She reflected on all the times he helped her on with her coat, and rested his hands on her shoulders for an extra, albeit brief, moment. She brought to mind all the little gestures that made her tummy do a little flip-flop and her heart skip a beat – she thought about them and recognized them as the beginnings of something more, something outside of "brotherly" affection. *This really has been building for a long time*, she thought. *And this is new territory for us. I really need to take some time with all this.*

Before she moved on to anything else, she needed a little divine direction. She set her empty coffee cup aside and reached for her well-worn Bible. She sifted through the pages and skimmed some of the highlighted passages which gave her a contented feeling. All those highlighted sections, notes in the margins and underlines were part of her journey. Much of that had actually been with Ricky and Jackson during their study times together.

Bible study and prayer can be such an intimate experience, Caroline thought as she smiled and recalled many of the times she and Ricky had prayed together. She was so thankful that their relationship was firmly grounded in the Lord.

She suddenly sat forward. *Even our prayer time reflects what's been happening,* she thought as she replayed moments from their singles group over the past year. Often times their group broke up into pairs or smaller groups for prayer. Jackson, Rick and Caroline had made a point of praying with others in an effort to build friendships and accountability outside of their little circle.

Over the past year, however, Rick had begun pairing up with Caroline more often during such prayer times. She didn't think anything of it at the time considering the year they'd had. *Wow! All that time You were knitting us even closer together, Lord.*

Encouraged by the Word, she began to pray earnestly for the needs of the day, the requests of her two most important guys and for wisdom.

Caroline stood up to stretch and noted that she had just enough time for a quick shower before heading to her studio for the day. Thankfully, her studio was in the back yard.

Caroline had spent her high school years dabbling in photography before she discovered that she not only had a passion for the art, but she had a keen eye for it as well. She worked on some small jobs for church and school taking photos for brochure projects. When it came time for college Caroline knew she wanted to study both photography and God's word.

When Caroline found a private Christian university where she could accomplish both photography and Biblical studies, it felt like a true gift. She worked hard during her four year undergraduate career earning a Bachelor in Science in Art with a minor in Biblical Studies. By the time she graduated, she had amassed quite a portfolio of professional work and established a rather extensive client base. She was inspired to formalize her entrepreneurial venture.

Many hours were spent in prayer and discussion before her parents decided to convert the oversized garden 'shed' in the backyard into a functional studio. Between the exposure she received from her excellent work at school showcasing her talent for landscape photography and the client base she had already built, her calendar filled up quickly with photo shoots and graphic design projects. She was humbled by the success of her business and was so thankful to the Lord for His gift of provision. It also gave her such joy to work in nature, sharing her love of the outdoors with others through her photography.

The previous night she'd finalized a series of photos from a shoot she had done earlier in the day in the snow at a local nature sanctuary. She'd had an exhilarating day watching the wildlife and indulging in a little easy climbing and hiking while she captured the natural activity and beauty of the space. Since the couple who ran the sanctuary lived in her same neighborhood, they had arranged to stop by just before lunch to go over the photos. They were anxious to put some current photos and information on their website to start off the New Year.

Caroline was lost in her mental planning of the day as she made her way toward the staircase. The sound of her phone's ring floated down the stairwell interrupting her thoughts. Once she connected with the sound, she sprinted up the rest of the stairs by twos in hopes of catching the phone before it went to voicemail. Diving across her bed, she grabbed her phone. Breathlessly, she answered. "Are you there? Did I catch you in time?"

Ricky's voice was quiet but jovial. "I'm here; you caught me. What were you doing?"

"I was just coming upstairs to take a quick shower when I heard your ring. I didn't want to miss you, so I sprinted up the stairs and flew across the bed." She tried to catch her breath as she climbed off the bed and walked to her closet.

A soft chuckle sounded through the phone. "That paints quite the picture. I've now got this vision of you sailing through the air in your fuzzy purple slippers with your robe flapping behind you like a cape. You crazy woman!" He chuckled again. "Anyway, I'm getting ready to go into my presentation but I wanted to call and let you know what time I'd be there to pick you up for dinner. I know you have a shoot this afternoon; can you be ready by six-thirty? I'm thinking a little nicer than business casual."

She smiled at his description of her flight across the bed while she did some quick mental calculating. "I can do that, yes. I'll be ready. And, Ricky?"

"Yea?" He asked with a smile; he loved hearing her say his name, he always had.

"You'll do great; you've totally got this. But I'll be praying for you just the same. See you tonight."

"Thanks, Sunshine. I'll see you at six-thirty." And with that, he disconnected his call.

* * * * *

The photos from the nature sanctuary came out beautifully. The light reflected off the snow and painted a lovely and serene landscape highlighting the peace and tranquility of winter at the sanctuary. It was exactly what they were looking for to accentuate the sanctuary and entice nature lovers to venture out on those cold winter days. A handful of photos were selected before the couple left her studio. Caroline forwarded the photos to the company that managed their website and finalized their paperwork.

She sat back in her chair and stared at the photo on her screen. It was a wide shot of the sanctuary grounds with the pond off-set from the middle and the nature center in the upper right corner. The rest of the photo displayed the trees, meadow and trailhead covered in a thick blanket of snow. It sure looked inviting. It was also a tricky shot to get. She'd had to climb just the right tree (she had tried three others) and straddle two branches. *Good thing I'm not afraid of heights,* she thought as she remembered her acrobatics of the previous day.

As she stared at the screen, she smiled as her thoughts drifted back to a picnic her singles small group from church had taken there during the summer. She and Rick had partnered up in the three-legged race. Although they did not win, far from it, they had more fun and laughed harder than they had all year. They had hopped and tumbled and rolled in the grass until they could hop and tumble and roll no further.

Remembering the day, she paused as she reflected on a particular moment on the ground after a tumble. She had grass sticking out of her hair and Rick gently pulled it out and ran his hand tenderly through her long, thick wavy hair. It was only a moment; so brief she had pushed it aside as a figment of her imagination. But it was there – a moment when time moved in slow motion and there was a look she couldn't explain and a rush of excitement coursed through her when her heart seemed to skip a beat. *It was there even then,* she thought and smiled.

As she thought of Rick, her fingers began playing

with the charm hanging around her neck. It was a beautiful and delicate gold and diamond sunburst on a simple gold chain. "A little sunshine for my Sunshine," he had said when he gave it to her on her birthday earlier that year. She had worn it every day since.

Her thoughts returned to the present and she closed the file on her screen. *I'd better focus, there's much to do today.* The rest of her day would be dedicated to her three o'clock photo shoot. She pushed back her chair and got busy cleaning her studio.

Caroline seldom held a photo shoot in her studio anymore. On the rare occasion she did a portrait shoot, it was outdoors in the country, the city, a field, you name it. However, more than two feet of snow on the ground did not allow for great accessibility for a wheelchair, so the couple, an acquaintance from church, asked for an in-studio session. She'd gone out earlier in the week shopping for a few new props and a new backdrop. She would be taking the couple's engagement pictures. If all went well, she might even receive the contract for their wedding in the late spring.

Caroline returned to her desk to print off the checklist for the shoot. Her list ready, it was time to grab a bite to eat, set up the shop, and sweep and salt the walkway from the drive. Time was ticking and three o'clock would chime all too soon.

CHAPTER 3

By four-thirty, her clients were gone. Reflecting on the session, she could not imagine having had more fun. What a treat to share in someone's love and joy. Not having to put the squash on her own burgeoning feelings may have added to the joy of the afternoon.

Caroline tidied up her studio and downloaded her photos into a new file to be sorted at a later time. She answered a handful of phone calls. Two resulted in new client consults scheduled for late January and three went on the calendar as photo shoots for the first week of February. Her final call was to her roommate from college. The two had worked hard to maintain their friendship since graduation, despite the distance between them.

She picked up on the third ring. "Hey there roomie!" Her voice held a smile.

Caroline smiled. *We will forever be roomies.* "Hi Annalise. I got your message. I only have a couple of minutes, but I wanted to connect before I shut down for the day."

"If I didn't know any better, I'd say it sounds like you have a hot date," Annalise teased.

Caroline remained silent, not sure how to respond.

"You do! You have a hot date! Okay, roomie, spill."

Caroline took a breath. "Well, actually, Ricky and I are…"

"I knew it!" Annalise burst in without letting Caroline finish. "I knew you two would end up together."

"You did not," Caroline countered.

"Did, too!" came Annalise's brilliant comeback.

"Since when?"

Annalise calmed her voice. "Oh, I don't know, but something's happened this year and you've changed how you talk about him. When I've prayed for you lately, I see Rick's face." She paused for a moment. "Okay that didn't sound so weird in my head, sorry. Anyway, I'm glad to hear this. What are you doing tonight?"

Caroline smiled at Annalise's jumble of words, but she was encouraged by her support. "We're going out to dinner. It would seem there is much for us to talk about."

"Well, I will look forward to hearing what the outcome is after Christmas. Which is why I called. I wanted to say Merry Christmas since I'll be out of touch mostly with family stuff for the next week or so. But then I want a good old-fashioned update."

"We will. And Merry Christmas to you, too. Have a wonderful time with your family and tell them I said hello."

"Will do, roomie. Have fun tonight and have a great Christmas."

Caroline smiled as she pressed the disconnect button. Annalise was a great friend and she would look forward to a long talk with her after the holiday.

Looking at the clock she noted the time. *Five twenty-three – plenty of time.* Satisfied, she prepared to leave. She could not remember the last time it was so easy to close up shop. The lights went out to the sound of the alarm's arming beep as Caroline locked the door and made her way back to the house.

At six-thirty the door-bell chimed. *Right on time.* She paused as she crossed the floor and looked at the door. *But since when does he use the bell? That's sweet.* She opened the door to see Ricky, hidden behind a beautiful bouquet of white calla lilies, purple hydrangea and purple lilacs.

"Beautiful flowers for a very beauti..." His voice trailed off and his breath was taken away by the vision before him. "Wow, Caroline. You look… amazing." For the past several months, maybe even the whole year, he had been seeing her through fresh eyes. It never failed to catch him unaware.

She wore the tailored red dress she knew he liked. It

was not often she had occasion to wear it, but she thought the night's activity qualified. From the look on his face, she knew she had guessed correctly. Even in heels, at 6'1" Rick still had to lean down as he placed a soft kiss on her cheek after he walked in the door.

He couldn't take his eyes off her. *She really is a vision*, he thought. He also realized that it was the first time it had been okay for him to openly admire her outside the confines of brotherly affection. He did not need to stop his thoughts, although he did need to keep them in check. He did not need to stuff down his feelings; he finally had permission to fully explore them. *This is new,* he thought. *What do I say?*

Rick had changed out of his work slacks and button down shirt into his midnight blue, pin-striped suit with a cranberry shirt and holly berries Christmas tie. Although she liked him best in jeans and a t-shirt or fitted sweater, he still took her breath away with how handsome he was. H*e always could fill out a suit like a model.* "The flowers are beautiful, Ricky. Thank you," she said nervously. "I think there's a vase hidden somewhere in the back room, if you'll help me get it down*?" I've known this man for almost fifteen years, why do I feel so unsure of myself?* "Ricky?"

He shook his head and re-focused his eyes. He looked and felt a little shell-shocked. "Flowers. Vase. Right. Of course. Lead the way." *Good grief! You sound like an idiot!*

But, Yowza! And, pull yourself together Richard! Remember who you are. Oh, Lord, what am I doing? Please help me out here. He followed her down the hall with roving eyes, admiring every inch of her along the way.

In the back room they slowly wound their way through yet another maze of boxes until Caroline pointed out a medium-sized box on the top of a box tower. She leaned back against another stack of boxes to allow room for him to pass. As he neared her, she could see a hunger in his eyes that ignited a rush of energy through her body and a longing deep within.

Rick looked at her with a passion he had not felt in a long time and an intensity that he had never experienced. The closer he got to her, the more he felt the heat and electricity between them. As he eased his body next to hers as they attempted to trade positions in the narrow path, Rick moved to put his hands on her waist. Only then did he realize that he still held the bouquet of flowers. With a shock he took in the scene.

Suddenly his mind and his focus cleared, as if emerging from a trance. *Major save there.* He looked down at the flowers, then into her eyes and smiled nervously. "You might want to hold on to these." Their hands touched as he passed her the flowers. Each of them caught their breath as they both felt the surge that raced through their bodies.

They had almost forgotten their purpose there.

Acutely aware of their closeness, Caroline blinked and tried to clear her head. "Why, uh, why don't I take these into the kitchen? I'll have them unwrapped by the time you bring in the vase." Without waiting for a response Caroline smiled, slipped out of the little path, turned toward the door and hustled out of the room. Rick watched her disappear from view.

* * * * *

Caroline needed a few minutes to gather her wits. She knew her attraction to Rick had grown, but the feelings that stirred within her in that back room were unlike anything she'd felt before. *That was almost explosive*. Suddenly she felt very childish, like an inexperienced schoolgirl. *With as many women as Rick has been with over the years, certainly this is nothing new for him.* Flooded with doubts, she inwardly chastised herself for being so foolish. *I'm not a schoolgirl, I'm a grown woman. And we are making a conscientious choice to pursue a new kind of relationship. He's an amazing man. A man I want to spend time with.*

She would never compromise her values or her convictions to keep up with other relationships from his past. *No, we will keep everything about our relationship pure, it will be above reproach.* She could not walk out of the house acting that way. *We need to talk.*

* * * * *

Rick sank to the floor, dropping his head in his hand. *What am I doing?* He figured the next step would be pretty easy. He had known Caroline for years; they already knew each other's stories. He'd spent time with plenty of women in the past, but he had never experienced anything even close to the magnetism and depth of feeling he had for Caroline. All the pent up and repressed feelings of the past year acted like they had a mind of their own and they were going to explode!

Inwardly Rick cried out to God; he really didn't know what else to do. He had not pursued any woman romantically since becoming a Christian six years ago. And Caroline was no ordinary woman. He knew exactly what he wanted out of their time together. Faced with the reality of taking her on a real date, Rick came face to face with his ugly past. An old default response had awoken and tempted him to behave in a way he'd long thought himself to have grown beyond.

He knelt down on the floor of that back room and had a heart-to-heart talk with God. Like a curtain rising on a play, Rick came to the full understanding of his quiet times in God's word as it related to yet another aspect of his life. *I'm really not that man I used to be; I am changed.* He could not leave the house without sharing with Caroline. *We need to talk.*

CHAPTER 4

Refocused and determined, Caroline was almost finished separating the flowers when Rick walked into the kitchen carrying a beautiful crystal vase, already filled with water from the bathroom down the hall. He looked as if a peaceful calm had washed over him.

"We need to talk." They both said at the same time. They looked at each other a little startled and then laughed nervously.

Rick placed the vase on the counter, stepped back to grab the nearby step stool, and sat down. "Ladies first, please."

She told herself she would not fidget, but she did. Trying to hide her nervousness, she slid the vase over and began arranging the flowers as she spoke. "I'm sure this is all stuff you've experienced before, feelings you've felt before," she looked to the side with a sense of uncertainly, "things you've done, but this is all really new for me. Even my time getting to know Thom all those years ago, I never felt… like this."

She struggled to get one flower settled into position. "I've been trying to figure out how long ago it was that my feelings for you began to change and I can't. I don't know how long I've been denying this."

She set the vase aside, now fully arranged with the beautiful bouquet. Caroline picked up a cut piece of flower stem. She twisted it as she talked. She tried to look at him, but she could only bring herself to raise her eyes as far as his feet. "Now, all of a sudden, I'm faced with the opportunity to acknowledge what I feel and to explore it, and," she finally looked up at him, "to contemplate that you're feeling the same thing, and I'm overwhelmed. I've always loved you, Ricky, and now I'm looking at that with a new kind of love and I'm, I'm kind of terrified."

As she continued, she could feel herself trembling, but she had to get out all of her thoughts. "I think you know me and my faith and my commitments and convictions well enough to know that if we walk out that door together, we're choosing a path that there's no going back from. And it's a very… conservative path," she blushed at the implication. "If we mess this up, Ricky, we mess up everything. And I'm not like the girls you've dated before."

She looked at him with severity and concern. "Are you sure you really want to do this?" she finished with a rush. *Oh, he's going to think I'm so childish.* That took every ounce of courage she had. Now that it was out there, there really was no going back. Whatever happened from that moment on, everything had already changed. Caroline tried to breathe as she waited, the flower stem now a limp and twisted mess.

Rick sat there for a moment, watching her watching him, as he let all that she had said sink in. He formulated his response. It must have felt like an eternity of silence for her, but he needed the moment before he began. Looking directly at her, he said. "What I really want to do right now is walk over there and hold you in my arms and kiss you. Actually, I *want* to do whole lot more than that, so that's why I'm just going to sit over here instead."

There was a playfully mischievous glint in his eye and smile on his face. However Rick saw Caroline shift her weight uncomfortably as she looked away. He breathed out a heavy sigh and continued, his voice sincere. "First of all, I owe you an apology. Jackson and I both do. See, we've been talking and praying about this for the past, what, six weeks. And that's after it took me about two months or so to work up the nerve to approach him. And that's after I wrestled with these feelings for, I really don't know how long before finally accepting what I was, in fact, feeling."

Caroline's gaze rested once more on Rick as he spoke. She tried to gauge his intentions and feelings by watching his body language and the look he gave her.

Rick went on. "Now here I am dropping this bomb on you that I don't want to be your brother anymore, I'd much prefer to, well, ultimately be your lover since there's only one destination this path will lead us. And I also know that you will only ever have one lover in your life, so I know exactly what I'm saying. So, first, Caroline, I'm asking if you will forgive me for selfishly pursuing this for so long without approaching you to consider how you might feel?" He waited quietly while he watched her process what he'd said.

She wanted to focus on all that he had said; to linger over certain words, but he was asking her for forgiveness. That was what needed attention. *I can't get distracted by... lover.* She tried to swallow a lump forming in her throat. *Not right now, right now...* With a kindness in her eyes he had come to count on, she said, "I could never begrudge you the time you needed to work through your feelings. And I'm glad you had Jackson to talk and pray with. I've had the amazing privilege of watching your faith and your commitment grow and overtake you. If forgiveness is what you ask for, I freely give it."

He smiled. "Thanks, Sunshine." She always amazed him. He began again, with a twinge of regret in his countenance. "I jumped a pretty big hurdle for myself back there a few minutes ago. Which leads me to a confession. I was seriously tempted back there. Those old Rick thoughts came flooding over me and I felt like I was going to explode. When you walked out of the room I literally knelt down on the floor and cried out to the Lord. I really didn't know anything else to do."

Rick shifted on the stool. "See, I didn't like those old thoughts, I don't like who I used to be, I don't ever want to be anything like him again, and I thought I'd grown passed all that. Moving forward I hate that my old self may have tainted what you and I *could* be. On the floor in that back room I was able to see and apply the truth that 'I've been made new' to this part of my life, too. I know with absolute certainty that I really am not *that* guy anymore and I never will be."

His face glowed with the joy he felt as he shared with her. *I can't imagine sharing all this with anyone else.* He continued, "I only pray that you can forget all about that old guy and only see the new man that God has been shaping me into. I really want to be the man you can turn to and lean on and trust with… with everything. I've been learning what it means to be the spiritual head of a home and a spiritual leader. Whether my home and family is a quantity of one or ten, I've surrendered this to God, too."

Caroline was filled with pride for how Rick was growing so strong in his walk with the Lord. His vulnerability and honesty with her was just what she needed to hear at that moment.

Rick lowered his head, rubbed his hands over the top of his pants and slowly stood. Covering the space to the counter that separated them in two short strides, he stood before her, his hands covering hers on the countertop. *She's shaking.* He slowly and gently began rubbing his thumb over her hand. They looked intently into each other's eyes as he continued. "And finally, you are right, Caroline. You aren't like any of the other <u>girls</u> I've spent time with. You are the most amazing <u>woman</u> I've ever known."

Caroline blushed as he spoke. She tried to concentrate on his words as she felt the warmth of his hands on hers.

"You are a woman of integrity; a woman of grace; a woman of incredibly alluring sex appeal;" he flashed her another mischievous smile, "a woman of wisdom; a woman of adventure. The intensity of the feelings I have for you terrifies me, too, because, believe it or not, I've never felt *anything* like this. Am I sure I want to walk this path? Caroline, I'm already on it; I'm already fully committed to it and to you. I know there's no going back, and at this point, frankly, I wouldn't even want to try. My question for you now is, do *you* want to do this?"

Caroline was overwhelmed, but her shaking had subsided and she had a renewed encouragement for what the two of them could be. She realized that it was the touch of his hands on hers that had ultimately quieted her anxiety. She still had a lump in her throat and did not trust her words, so she looked up, smiled a smile that made her eyes sparkle like emerald gems and nodded her head.

"I know this is going to sound totally corny and probably incredibly cliché, but I'm going to say it anyway. In light of all that's happened here tonight, would you mind if we took a minute to pray?"

Finding her voice, Caroline responded. "Because I know us like I do, it's not corny. I'd actually like that very much. And I'm very glad you led us here." *Thank You for the strength in his leadership, Lord.*

Standing in the kitchen, holding hands over the island counter, Rick led them in a brief prayer. Honestly, he couldn't think of a better way to spend any part of their evening. *Next time, we'll start here. I guess I'm still learning, huh, Lord.*

Holding her hands, he lifted them and began to circle around the counter. "Come here, you." She gave him a demure and questioning look as she cocked her head. He knew all too well what she was silently asking. "Trust me. I have more than enough self-control to hold you in my arms now. Come here."

With her arms around his waist, he enveloped her in

the same loving embrace that took their breath away earlier in the morning. He held her for only a moment. The moment was all too brief, but he knew that any longer and red flashing sirens would begin to spin in his head.

"Are you still up for dinner?" He asked. As if on cue, her stomach rumbled loudly causing them both to burst out laughing.

Caroline grabbed her mid-section and looked at Rick with dancing eyes, "I guess that's a yes from my stomach, and a yes from me, too."

"We'd better be going if we have any hope of getting our table and not losing our night completely if Jackson comes home." Leading her to the foyer he helped her on with her coat before guiding her out the door to his Jeep.

*****

Little did the two of them know that Jackson had walked in just as their "talk" was getting underway. He had noticed Rick's Jeep out front and didn't want to disturb them, so he quietly came in the back door. Although he did not exactly mean to eavesdrop, he really didn't have anywhere to go without making his presence known, and it certainly was not the time for an interruption. So, he heard their whole discussion. It was rather insightful. Even through all of the talks he'd had with each of them separately over the past couple of months, he heard a few things there that he had not heard before from either of them. *Good thing he's got sufficient self-control; I'd hate to have to deck my own brother. And when did my sister get to be so beautiful, and dumb? What's with the insecurities? Hmm...*

CHAPTER 5

Rick found a place to park on the square and they walked the short distance to the steak house. Wednesday night with snow on the ground had not kept people at home. The sidewalks had been cleared of snow and salt was scattered in places that might be slick. Shoppers were bustling and the restaurant was teeming with diners. It was, after all, Christmastime and the town square was lit up and sparkling. The square always drew a large crowd at the holidays with shoppers eager to see the lights and decorations, as well as pick up their special gifts for family and friends.

Thankfully they were not late enough to have lost their table. The restaurant was running a little behind as well so when they arrived and checked in they were seated almost immediately. Close enough to a fireplace to hear the crackle of wood and the hiss of the flames, yet away from the bar and all the chatter and excitement, their table was perfect. As they settled in, an awkward silence passed between them. They each fidgeted in their seat like two-year olds, looking around for something to say.

Rick broke the awkward silence. "Oh, this is silly, Sunshine. It's not like we have to change who we are or even change how we interact with one another. Come on, this should be easy. We have plenty of things we can talk about. This is just a continuing on of our relationship, not the very beginning."

Caroline thought about that for a moment. "We're talking about a completely different type of relationship between us, with different hopes and expectations and even a different set of rules. We can't really expect to drop ourselves into the middle of what we hope we'll become, we do need to start at a new beginning."

A thoughtful silence fell between them as their waitress arrived to inform them of the specials and take their drink and appetizer orders. Rick had a hunch, but he did not want to be overly presumptuous, so he took the lead before ordering drinks and asked, "Is it an iced tea or wine night?"

"Iced tea, please."

With a knowing smile, Rick looked at their waitress and said, "Make it two, please, no lemon." *Just as I thought.* He knew her well. However, their night was going to be unlike any date he had ever been on. *Not that I'd call any of that dating.* After all, Caroline was unlike any woman he had ever spent time with and that was the most purposeful way he had ever approached spending his time. The term 'first date' had already taken on new meaning as he prepared for the next part of the journey. *I'm not sure just how prepared I am for this. But I know where we're headed and I'm sure we're going to get there.* He still felt entirely certain of that. Rick knew without a doubt that he wanted to spend the rest of his life with that woman at his side. And he was willing to find that new beginning to get them there. God things like that never ceased to amaze him.

"So, we already enjoy a very companionable friendship." Rick thought that was a good place to start finding their new beginning.

"And we already laugh at each other's bad jokes." She shot him a perky smile.

"Hey, who tells bad jokes? You certainly can't mean me!" he said with a mock pout.

"Oh, I know I mean both of us!"

Rick laughed and thought, *Yea, we'll be able to do this. Our foundation is solid, it won't fail us.* "We already actively pursue God's word together in study, discussion and prayer. There's no more firm foundation for any relationship than that. And it's something I'm looking forward to doing more of, just the two of us. Would you be interested in having some type of devotional time together?"

Caroline looked thoughtfully at Rick. Once again, past moments of the two of them huddled together, shoulder to shoulder or heads almost touching, praying flashed through her mind. *Those times have been so intimate,* she thought as a slight blush washed over her. "This is actually one of my favorite parts of our friendship. But, honestly, I love that we get to share this with Jackson. I've always felt it knits us together as family in the most unique and powerful way. This past year more than ever. I don't want to give that up. If Jackson were to find a woman he wanted to date or court, I hope that she'd join us during their courtship and be knit into our little family rather than take Jackson away from it."

"I do feel the same way, don't get me wrong. I'm just hoping to find a different balance, a new balance. That's not wrong, is it?" He sure hoped he was saying that right. Jackson would always be family and he never wanted to lose that.

She smiled. "No, not wrong; I think I understand. And I look forward to that one-on-one time, too, I just think that falls into a special intimacy category that's reserved for later. Not only would we benefit from another's input, it would also be a wise accountability practice during this season of our relationship." She could feel the flush in her cheeks deepen.

It was his turn to smile. “I can see that. We’ve always had an understanding between us, that type of accountability was never necessary, I guess. This is a big rule changer, isn’t it?”

“Just look at what happened earlier this evening. Although being open and honest about all of this will help, I think we would be wise to exercise a little prudence with accountability.”

Rick hedged slightly before continuing. “Can we put this in the ‘things to iron out as we go along’ category?”

“Are you making fun of me, Ricky?” She suddenly felt a drop in confidence again.

Quick to pick up on her insecurity, he hoped his response assuaged her appropriately. “Absolutely not,” he said as he reached for her hand. “I just mean that we’re not going to sort everything out perfectly tonight. This is a journey, not the destination. And we *can* have *fun* doing this, too, you know.”

His smile sparkled all the way to his eyes, reminding her just why she was there, with him. She averted her gaze and smiled. *You’re choosing each other, Caroline. He’s right. Lighten up a little and enjoy this.* “I’ve heard some of the newly married ladies at church talk about a couple’s devotional dealing with expectations. That might be a good place to start. How about I ask them about it? Would that be okay?"

"Sounds perfect," he smiled at her encouragingly and gave her hand a gentle squeeze. "I look forward to hearing what you find out."

Their appetizer tray arrived and they ate in thoughtful silence after Rick led them in a simple grace. Melodic Christmas music was playing in the background. When "Mary, Did You Know" came on they both stopped and smiled at each other. That had always been Caroline's favorite song during the holiday. It only took Rick a heartbeat to decide. Putting down his fork and laying aside his napkin, he stood and held out his hand to Caroline. "May I have this dance?"

Caroline blushed and shyly looked around the room. A few heads began to turn at his movement. "They don't do that here, Ricky."

Never one to be concerned with conforming to a set boxed-in standard, he lowered his voice and urged her. "Come on, Sunshine. What are they going to do, ask us to leave? Dance with me. There are more than fifty chaperones in this room. I promise to be a perfect gentleman."

With a smile that lit up her whole face, she placed her hand in his and stood. They joined together in a quiet, simple dance at the side of their table. It was the perfect romantic gesture, and she felt like the most special woman in the world. Smiling up at him, those fifty chaperones disappeared into the fringe beyond her peripheral vision and she had eyes only for Rick.

They held a tight circle at the side of their table as they danced slowly to the music. With one arm firmly around her waist, he held her close, eliminating any space between them. In his other hand he held hers, rested upon his chest. With her left arm draped around his shoulder, she took in every movement. The air between them seemed to have escaped and they remained in their own personal bubble.

As the music neared its end she felt his hand glide up her back firmly as he made a slight step to the side and finished the dance with a gentle dip. Her head fell back and she captured her giggle before it escaped. Raising her back up, he held her close once more and planted a kiss on her cheek before whispering "Thank you" in her ear.

As the room came back into focus she noticed several other couples finishing a dance at their table before they all returned to their seats. The remaining diners and lingering wait staff offered a soft applause. Then the room returned to its usual quiet din and Rick and Caroline enjoyed every last moment of the experience as they, too, returned to their appetizers and their meal was served.

"Do you remember the first time you agreed to be my dance partner?" Rick asked.

Caroline almost choked at the memory. “Considering I was almost the biggest scandal at school and I didn’t have a clue what I was doing, yes, I remember. I still can’t believe you talked me into that competition.”

Rick laughed. “I can’t believe we took third place.”

“I still have that little trophy somewhere,” said Caroline.

“After I took you home, you told me if I ever wanted to dance with you again, I’d better get us some lessons,” Rick laughed.

Caroline smiled. “And the next Saturday night we were at our first class. I couldn’t believe you did that.”

“You know, I had a hard time convincing Jackson it was no big deal, just something fun, but not throw-away fun – long term fun. I swear, he watched me like a hawk for months.”

“And he grilled me after every class. Once he saw that charity dance-a-thon that you agreed to do with me he backed off. I never understood why, but I was glad to be rid of the third degree.”

“Yea, he and I had quite the talk after that one. It took me a while, but he finally believed that I had no romantic or flirtatious designs on you; that you were the one woman in my life I could just be myself around and I wanted to dance with you. Although I think it took longer than it appeared, he finally believed me."

"And now look at us," Caroline grinned.

"Yes, indeed, look at us now," Rick sat up and smiled. "We move together like Fred and Ginger."

She smiled shyly at his compliment. "That's not exactly what I meant, but I've always liked dancing with you, too."

He reached for her hand. "I know." He kissed her hand. "And I can't imagine having any other partner."

After several moments, Rick returned to their earlier conversation. "Let's see. Somewhere along the line we've learned how to listen to each other and hear out the other's opinion or position on a matter before either agreeing with further input or offering a refute or rebuttal."

Leaning over to look around his dinner plate, Caroline asked with a chuckle, "Alright, Ricky, do you have some kind of list you're playing from tonight?" She started to peek into his inside jacket pocket.

He playfully slapped her hand away. "Well, not a written one. You know I work best with a mental list. Why? Don't you have a list with you somewhere?" One eyebrow raised, he looked at her with a knowing smile.

She stopped and stared at him. He had her, and they both knew it. She shook her head and reached into her purse to pull out a folded piece of notebook paper. "How'd you know?"

"Because I know you." Once again his eyes gleamed. "I wouldn't expect anything less. Well, don't start a shy routine now, fire away."

"Honestly, you've been answering many of my questions just in our conversation already." Caroline looked at him with an innocent smile. "I didn't want to upset the flow."

"Well, you have to play fair," Rick said playfully. Continuing with a more serious yet honest tone, he said, "You might be getting your answers, but I'd still like to know the questions. I want to know what you're asking, what you're looking for specifically. I have some questions I'm pretty sure I know the answers to simply because I know you so well, but I want to know definitively, so I'll be asking them so you can answer yourself. That's part of the 'clear expectations' category."

Caroline realized where he was coming from. "I hadn't thought of it like that. I'm sorry I wasn't playing fair."

Their conversation didn't falter all through the night as they talked out their 'lists' of expectations and questions. Dinner turned into after-dinner coffee, which turned into dessert, which was followed by a second cup of coffee. So focused on each other, huddled together talking, they had barely registered their waitress throughout the evening, and time became irrelevant.

CHAPTER 6

Sitting back for a moment to stretch their shoulders, their eyes took in the emptiness around them. No other diners remained and the fire had been reduced to embers.

"I think we've closed down the place. What time is it, anyway?" Rick asked as he pulled out his phone to check the time. "Oh, my, it's after eleven. I think we'd better pay our bill and let these people close up." He looked at Caroline with a guilty grin.

Caroline responded with her own shy grin. "I guess we kind of got lost in our own conversation." She reached for her purse and said, "If you'll excuse me for a moment, I'll duck into the ladies room real quick and be ready to go."

They both stood and Caroline made her way toward the restrooms in the back. Returning to his seat, their waitress appeared with their check. They exchanged a few words as he quickly handed off his credit card and leaned back in his seat to wait. A contented smile played about his lips as he gazed blindly into the burning embers. *Thank you for bringing us to this night, Lord. Now, help me be the man You want me to be, for her, and for You.*

Their waitress returned with the receipt and Caroline was close behind. Rick stood briefly as she reclaimed her seat before filling in the tip to settle their bill. Caroline glanced over the table as he wrote in the amount, one hundred dollars, with a note to the side that read “A Merry and Blessed Christmas to you!” and drew a little smiley face. He then filled in the total before signing the slip. Setting it aside he looked up to see Caroline smiling at him.

He felt like he’d been caught with his hand in the proverbial cookie jar just before dinner was to be served. With lighthearted defensiveness he said, “It’s Christmas. And we completely monopolized this table for the whole night. *And* we weren’t very aware of anything around us. And… it’s Christmas!” He stood up to retrieve her coat.

She stood and slipped her arms into the sleeves and turned to face him, still smiling. “I just appreciate seeing your generous spirit. That’s all.” She collected her purse once more and they made their way to the door saying “Good night,” and “thank you,” as they exited.

Stepping out into the wintery night, they were met with a rush of cold air. Caroline shivered and drew her coat a little tighter. Rick stepped to her side and put his arm around her. Looking down, he asked, “Are you warm enough for a walk around the square before we head home, or are you ready to leave?"

She reached into her pockets to pull out her gloves and ear muffs. Looking up she said, "A walk with you would be great. I'm good." As she bundled up, she added, "I know the shops are closed, but I always enjoy looking at the window decorations. I love the old-fashioned feel it evokes. Plus, with no decorations at our home, or yours for that matter, I need to live a little vicariously."

With her hands warmly sheathed in her gloves, Rick reached down to entwine his fingers with hers. He lifted their hands and kissed her fingers as he smiled down at her.

Feeling a little breathless, Caroline bit the inside of her cheek as she smiled up at him.

Turning, they strolled, hand-in-hand, along the sidewalk, stopping to enjoy each window along the way. At that late hour, they were two of only a handful of pedestrians out on the square, which made for a very peaceful promenade.

"I hope you don't take this the wrong way," Rick began, "but I think I've had business contract negotiations that were less intense. Not intense as in adversarial, more, hmm. . ." He looked up, trying to find the right phrase. "This is just the most unique and purposeful way I could've ever thought about approaching a relationship. I continue to be amazed at how much God has changed my approach to everything - my expectations, my desires and my hopes. As uncomfortable as following His leading and direction can be sometimes, I'm always gratified at how He blesses the outcome."

She had stiffened a little and slowed her pace. "So, this is like a contract negotiation for you? Like… a business deal?"

He stopped and turned her to face him. There it was again. He could see insecurity, doubt and even hurt in her eyes. *Where has all this insecurity come from? This is my confident, tree climbing, conceal-carrying, trail-blazing, take-charge woman. I'll need some help to figure this one out, Lord.*

His voice was soothing. "No, Sunshine. See, I said 'don't take this wrong'; that should've been your clue that I'd *say* it all wrong. No, what we're talking about is more like a… a covenant than a contract, that's much more important, and," he wrapped his arms around her and grinned, "*much* more intimate. I'll just leave it at 'intense' and stop digging a hole I fear I'll never find my way out of."

She blushed, shook off her insecurities and doubts, rested her hands on his arms and realized that he was right. "I'm sorry, Ricky. You're right, really. It has been a pretty intense night. But a good night, I think?" Her eyes were inquisitive.

He pulled her tight. “A very good night, indeed.”

“Are we really doing this? On the same page, all synced up?” The look in Caroline’s eyes was now hopeful.

Rick could not remember ever feeling so content or certain. “I can’t think of anything more I’d like to do than sweep you off your feet and build a life together. On the same page and synced? I think so. I think I’ve heard your requests and expectations clearly, and I think I’ve properly agreed. And I think I’ve made my intentions and my expectations clear?”

Shyly she nodded. “I think so. And I acknowledge, and agree.” She could feel herself fading into his arms.

He slid his hand up, along her neck, under her chin; just like he’d done that morning. His words were low and thick as he leaned down a little closer to her and said, “Then there’s only one more thing to do.” She closed her eyes, leaned her head into his hand, and. . .

All of a sudden he’d scooped her up into his arms and he was spinning them in circles. She clung to his neck and the two laughed aloud as he spun her around. Life seemed to move in slow motion even as the world around her blurred. She was enraptured by the freedom and security she felt being held in his arms as they indulged in a moment of youthful spontaneity. Before they got too dizzy, he slowed and came to a stop. Gently, he released her legs and held her as she found her own footing, both of them still laughing.

He stepped back, holding onto her hands, their laughter turning to quiet mirth. Their eyes still sparkling, he said, “Come on, Sunshine, let’s finish our walk.” And once again, hand-in-hand, they made their way the rest of the way around the square to Ricks’ Jeep and on to home.

▪▪

CHAPTER 7

"Why did I agree to have breakfast with you this early?" Caroline said groggily as she stumbled into the living room still feeling half asleep.

Jackson poured her a cup of coffee and grinned. "How late did you get home? I fell asleep around eleven watching a movie in my room. I never heard you."

Welcoming the cup she said, "Thank you. It was about twelve-thirty or so, I think, when I came in. Were you waiting up for us?" She wrapped her hands around the cup and let the aroma envelope her.

"No, I went to my room so I'd be out of your way if you guys wanted to spend any time here. I didn't know what your plans were, exactly, but I know there was a lot to talk about. I didn't figure you needed me around. But even in my room there'd still technically be a chaperone here for you crazy kids." He grinned at her playfully.

She made a face at him and stuck out her tongue. At the same time, she also loved that her brother understood her values, now more than ever, and always looked out for her. "We went to dinner at the steak house on the square and actually shut the place down. We never realized just how late it had gotten. Dinner was nice, but really, it was the company and conversation that made it special. Afterward we took a stroll around the square to look at all the decorated windows. It was a good night. Ricky's word was 'intense'. But in a good way."

Flipping the omelets, he asked, "So, did you get through each of your lists?"

Caroline snickered. He knew them both so well. "Exactly how long have you been talking with Rick about this? And exactly why have you taken *his* side and had *his* back, oh brother of <u>mine</u>?"

He pulled out two paper plates and two plastic utensil sets. "First of all, I'm always on your side, little sister, never doubt that. And before I say anything else, I have a confession to make. I actually came home last night while you guys were still here. I didn't want to disturb you so I came in the back door. Honestly, I figured you'd be heading out the front door as I came in the back so it wouldn't be a big deal. Turns out I was wrong. You were in the kitchen putting flowers in a vase. Since I didn't want to interrupt, and there was nowhere for me to go, I ended up hearing your conversation before you left." He paused to look at her.

"Oh." Is all she said.

He plated the omelets and began to add some sour cream and salsa to both. "Something I heard Rick say set me thinking last night and I realize he was right. I do owe you an apology. I knew something was different quite some time ago; there was that 'something in the air' kind of thing. Rick had been acting weird for a while and there had been silent pauses among us all that I didn't really pay much attention to. After all, why should I? So, in typical 'male' fashion (so I'm told), I was clueless."

He handed her a plate and held out a hand. She placed her hand in his and they bowed their heads while Jackson said a simple grace. Jackson wanted to finish what he had to say before diving into his breakfast, so after their 'amen', he continued.

"Anyway, once Rick actually approached me and he and I started talking things through, he asked me to pray with him. I'm sorry that I hid all this from you; that I kept secrets about feelings and agendas that concerned you from you. I was trying to give Rick the time he needed to move forward at his own pace, but I didn't consider that it might be a betrayal to you, too. I will be more conscientious about how Rick and I talk in the future. Will you forgive me?"

Caroline's initial discomfort at hearing that he had heard the conversation in the kitchen the night before quickly disappeared. She could see and hear his contrition and his love for her, and Rick. She so appreciated his honesty with her. “Thank you, Jackson. And, of course I forgive you. I don’t believe you’d do anything to purposely hurt me. I guess this is all new territory that we need to figure out. Let’s just do it together from now on. Deal?”

“Deal. Let’s eat.” They both dove in, the ensuing silence simply a reflection of the two indulging their appetites.

Paper and plastic certainly made mealtime cleanup a breeze. Working together, they made short work of the little that was left to do. With a second cup of coffee in hand, they headed for couch and chair to finish chatting.

Caroline began. “You’ve had quite a bit of time to process this whole idea of Ricky and me. How do you feel about all this?”

Jackson thought for a moment about how to start. “When Rick first approached me, I think I surprised him with my response. I wasn’t mad; and I know he was afraid I would be. After all, no one makes moves on my sister – least of all any friend of mine. And he’s family. From that first holiday he spent with us, he’s been family.”

He shifted in his seat slightly. “Now, if he’d tried anything like this much sooner, I think I would’ve been mad, and disappointed, like he’d betrayed me or something. But, honestly, it hasn't been that big of an adjustment to think about. When I watch the two of you, it actually seems like a natural fit. At this point, I'm good with this. That being said, I'm still going to look out for my little sister. I hope you can handle that."

Jackson would forever be her brother. Their relationship had grown in so many ways over the years. It was a fun and solid and curious blend of friendship, loyalty, sibling angst, honesty, antagonism, encouragement and love. She never failed to thank the Lord for the blessing of their relationship – it was a gift she did not take for granted.

Caroline smiled at her brother. "I've always counted on that." She let out a tired sigh. "This feels crazy, like we're headed down taboo lane. And I'm not exactly what I would consider Ricky's 'type'."

Jackson was quick to own up to his part of that statement. "That taboo part is my fault, I guess. I'm sorry that's been a stumbling block for getting to this point."

Caroline looked at him thoughtfully. "I don't see it that way. God's had His plan, and we're discovering it all at just the right time. I figure there's stuff we've all had to do or work through to be ready for this now."

Jackson looked at her for moment. She never ceased to surprise him. "That's why I like talking with you, Caroline, you always show me something from a really healthy perspective."

"That's what *big* sisters are for, don't ya know." She shot him a sassy grin.

Jackson shot her a look only a loving brother could get away with. "Nice. Seriously, though, can you tell me? How you do feel? I know we've talked before about relationships in general but what *are* your feelings for Rick? Do you love him?"

She sighed. A shy smile quickly passed over her face. "I've always loved Ricky. Am I 'in love' with him? That's part of what I need to sort out. I know that, at some point this past year, my feelings for him have definitely changed. But I never gave myself permission to consider anything romantic. Why would I? Taboo, remember?"

Jackson nodded.

"Learning, now, that his feelings have changed too, has been a mix of frightening and exhilarating."

"So where are you after your date last night?" A mischievous smile spread across his face. "Do I need to greet him at the door the next time he comes over in my overalls, cleaning the shot gun with the .45 on the coffee table?" Jackson attempted his best Jeb Clampett impression. "Time to vet this here new pro-spective boy-friend a' yourn? Gotta find out his in-tenshons!" He was enjoying himself a little too much.

"Oh, stop it! And don't you dare, Jackson!" She tossed a chair pillow across the room at him.

He laughed out loud and tried to dodge the pillow. It hit him square in the face. "Okay, okay. I'll just wear my regular clothes," he continued with a low chuckle while Caroline rolled her eyes. Taking a deep breath to calm himself down, he started again. "Seriously, where are you two after last night?"

"Well, I've got to say, knowing that he'd already spoken with you before and that you were okay with this made taking this step burden free. I didn't feel like we were betraying you or our family unit that we've built." Her eyes expressed more than her words as she looked directly at him and said, "So, as weird as it may sound, thank you, Jackson."

Quietly, almost to himself, he answered, "I never thought I'd ever play that particular role for you, but it really was my pleasure." They both shared in the unspoken thoughts that filtered between them.

Returning to their conversation, Caroline said, "Well, we really did talk through our lists. We talked about expectations, what kind of new beginning this is, even new rules. He was very clear about his intentions, of which I believe you're already fully aware."

Again, Jackson nodded.

Caroline continued, "And Ricky formally asked for

permission to court me." She paused, thinking about the words she'd just spoken. "Gosh, saying that out loud sounds so silly. I'm thirty years old, run my own business, and live in the twenty-first century and I'm being courted. Do I need to check for a corset and hoop skirt hanging in my closet?"

Jackson laughed out loud. "I think you're safe, sis."

She shook her head to clear away the nineteenth century images. Returning to the present, she finished, "Anyway, I said yes."

Jackson rang out, "Finally! Just promise me that you won't start being all kissy face all the time. This single guy could very quickly feel like an unwanted third wheel."

Caroline quickly responded. "Oh, no, you won't have to worry about that. That's part of our agreement – no physical stuff. And we want the accountability, so we were kind of hoping you'd help us. Plus, what the three of us share is too valuable to both of us; we don't want to lose any of that."

With a more serious tone, Jackson said, "I guess we're all entering new territory with this. And, of course I'll help. For now, I should probably…" The familiar chime of the grandfather clock cut him off. Eight o'clock. "Like I was saying, I should probably get a move on. I've got some early meetings this morning before an afternoon of planning. Are we making up our Bible study tonight?"

"As far as I know, that's the plan. Ricky said he'd see me tonight. I'll call you if I find out anything more. Have a good day."

Standing, he pulled her into a big bear hug. "I love you, sis."

"I love you, too, Jackson."

CHAPTER 8

The house was all hers for the day. And with such an early start, she had plenty that she could accomplish. Caroline decided a quick quiet time was needed before diving into her to-do list. She picked up the empty coffee cups to dispose of them and grabbed her Bible. Skimming through Ephesians, the book the three of them had been studying that month, she reflected on several highlighted passages, before committing her day to prayer.

Caroline had already dressed for working in the kitchen before she stumbled downstairs for breakfast with Jackson. She had slipped into her 'stain and paint pants' and thrown on an old rust colored long-sleeved henley before pulling her thick tresses up in pigtails. Work clothes always felt the most comfortable.

Pleased with her readiness, Caroline headed to the stash of staining supplies. There were some new base cabinets set as a result of Jackson's night at home. It was time to do some staining. With a little 40's big band music playing to boost her energy level, she began her morning task.

Half way through the second coat of stain on the upper cabinets, Caroline's phone began to chime. A smile spread across her face and her heart skipped a beat. It was Ricky. She set her supplies down on the makeshift counter and dug the phone from her pocket.

"Good morning, Ricky!" came her cheerful greeting as she climbed down the step ladder to turn down the music.

"Good afternoon, Caroline. Do you have a moment?" Rick's voice was all business.

Afternoon? Hmm. "I'm in the middle of wet cabinets, but what can I do for you?" *Oops, that was the company line.* Rick's architectural firm was also a client and the two had worked out little cues to indicate when it was time to set aside familiarity and get down to business. Rick's tone clearly indicated his stress, and his choice of words told her that someone else was in the office.

"Do you remember the estate we finished designing last year? The construction finished just before the snow began to fall?"

Caroline thought for a moment to recall as many details as possible. "Yes, I remember. You indicated a desire for formal photos of the full finished project once everything was complete. We went over a pretty comprehensive list of what you'd like a while back. We've been in a holding pattern since October."

Rick was pleased with her recall. "That's the one. While I was in my meeting this morning we got the call with the all clear for the photo shoot. Their agent is bringing by a key after lunch today. The only problem is they want it done before Christmas and they're having a large open-house on Saturday night."

I hate to dump all this on her, he thought, but he continued. "Marjory also just informed me that the deadline for entering this project for consideration for next fall's regional architectural magazine is the end of this month. Is there any chance you have the time to make this happen?"

Caroline looked at the clock. Twelve forty-five. *No wonder I'm hungry. It's well past lunchtime.* She had not planned on doing more than staining cabinets and sorting those engagement photos. She needed to clear her head, and get some food. She also noticed the stain dripping off the brush onto the counter.

Oh no. I'm dripping. Quickly, she responded to Rick. "May I call you back in ten minutes while I re-evaluate my schedule?"

Rick recalled her telling him that she had taken the day off to work on the kitchen and hated interfering. *She's probably dripping stain somewhere.* He turned to face the wall of windows that overlooked a small lake in the park-like business complex housing his offices. He let out a quiet sigh.

His voice a little softer, he answered her. "I'm sorry, Caroline, but I also just received a call that there's a problem at the construction site down by the marina and the owner is adamant that I come down immediately. I'm trying to arrange things so I can walk out the door."

He spoke even softer, "Take a moment, Caroline, but please don't hang up."

She knew he was trying not to be demanding or harsh. And she knew he was stressed. Her brain continued to work as she stalled with a question. "Are you alone?"

"No," he said resolutely.

"Can you clear the room?" she asked with a hint of mischief.

"I'd rather not." Rick's voice dropped an octave and the tension eased a little.

"I understand." She took a breath. "I'm stalling." Caroline tried not to grin while saying that, but she didn't succeed.

Rick grinned and more of the tension began to fade. Still trying to keep a little professionalism to his voice he continued. "I understand, that, too. I can have Tom and Caleb meet you out at the estate with the key and willing arms and backs to help with any re-staging you want."

Tom was the second architect Rick hired a little over a year ago. At a height of 5'8", his solid muscular build gave him a stocky appearance. His wavy brown hair and hazel eyes complemented an easy going yet focused personality. He was single but had a steady girlfriend, and was a year or so younger than Caroline. He'd proven to be a hard worker, creative and more than competent in all aspects of the job. He had become a true asset to the firm.

"Will there be anyone at the estate this afternoon?" Caroline looked down at her stain-covered pants. *At least everything is dry.*

"No. The message I received was that the decorator had finished and cleared out yesterday. They have not officially moved in so the place will be completely empty for the rest of the day today and tomorrow. They won't begin their party preparations until tomorrow evening."

Oh, who am I kidding here? he thought, finally giving up and losing all the formality left in his voice. "You and your stain covered jeans and pig-tails will be just fine." All the stressed-out business tone was gone and he smiled. *Man, she's good. Even if she says no, she's just what I needed at this moment.*

Her eyes and mouth flew open wide and she stood speechless for a brief moment. "How did you...?" She groaned. "Oh, never mind. Tomorrow is a definite no, so give me a half, better make that forty-five minutes to shut things down here and grab my notes from our original meeting and my gear before I head out." Her stomach let out a low growl. "Have your guys stop and buy me a pink berry power smoothie from the smoothie shop down the street from you and I'll meet them at the estate."

"A pink - berry - power - smoothie?" There was actual amusement in his voice now.

"Yep, that's what it's called. Don't laugh." She could hear him inquire of someone else in the room.

Returning to Caroline, Rick said, "Okay, Tom knows the place. And the estate is only fifteen minutes from you, so I'll have the two of them meet you there, with your smoothie, an hour from now."

Once everyone in the room heard Rick repeat the plan, they exited his office to prepare for the afternoon, each knowing what needed to be done.

Rick continued, "Caroline, you are the best. Thank you."

"Oh, you're not off the hook that easy, mister. The smoothie is from the guys, YOU are still going to owe me big time. I don't drop a staining project for just anyone, you know," Caroline said playfully.

Rick laughed. "Well, you got me there, Sunshine. How about we do Bible Study at your place? I'll bring the food for all of us and afterward I'll help you finish staining those cabinets. What do ya say?"

"Ooh, you got a deal, Ricky."

Rick was design, not detail finisher. He had never liked that tedious part of a project. When it came to his designs, he was meticulous and detailed, but the hands-on painting and staining just were not his forte'. Caroline knew his offer was a gift for her and she appreciated it.

The phone cradled in her shoulder, she finished pounding the lid on the stain can and put the brush into a plastic zipper bag. She turned off the music. Gathering her thoughts, she said, "And Rick?"

"Yes, Caroline?" he said formally.

"Whatever is going on at the construction site, you've submitted a solid plan and blueprint. I know your day just got flipped upside down, but go with the intent to encourage and clarify. When they're right on top of the problem it's hard to see the truth of the situation. You're coming in from a fresh perspective. So, take it in stride and draw on God's grace, wisdom and peace. You'll see, it'll still be a good day."

Any day I get to spend with you is a good day, he thought.

Rick was alone, now sitting at his desk looking at a photo of Caroline, Jackson and himself. He smiled and said quietly into the phone, "I knew I'd called the right person.

You sure know how to make everything better."

"Ah, yes. Bet-ter. Comtriya!" The two of them laughed at her reference to an old Stargate SG-1 episode. "Alright, if I'm going to make this shoot, I'd better get going."

With renewed energy, Rick responded. "Yea, me too. Sorry I can't be out there with you. I always enjoy watching you work. But, the client calls. I will see you tonight, though. I'll shoot for six, but I'll call if it'll be later. Would you be able to fill in Jackson?"

"I can do that. See you tonight." With one last good-bye, they disconnected their call.

CHAPTER 9

Caroline made quick work of the remaining cleanup in the kitchen. She left everything ready to resume the project later that night. A hustle up the stairs for her winter gear and she was out the back door to the studio. She'd had to learn the art and discipline of filing and paper work. For as detailed as she was about her lists and note taking for a project, filing was a task she had to work hard at maintaining. On such days, she was glad she remained diligent, and Rick no longer reprimanded her on the stacks and piles on her desk. Quickly finding what she needed, she grabbed her folder for the project and began the task of gathering her gear.

Thankful that the snow was not falling that afternoon, she was in her forest green Jeep Grand Cherokee headed to the estate right on time. While en route, she left Jackson a voice message detailing the events of the day and the plans for dinner and Bible study. She slipped her phone into her purse as she drove along the perimeter of the estate grounds.

The freshly fallen snow, untouched by vehicle or

pedestrian traffic, would make a breathtaking backdrop for the outdoor photos. She would start there, before she lost the best of the afternoon winter sun. Slowing to make her turn into the lane, she was the first in line, noticing two other vehicles pull in after her.

Caroline drove at a snail's pace up the lane, looking and calculating as she determined where to set up for the outdoor shots. What providence that she was first to turn into the lane. She controlled where the cars started and kept the lane as free from tracks as possible. Since she knew that no other cars or people would need the lane, she stopped right in the center and put the Jeep in park. Tom and Caleb followed close behind and did the same.

Caleb climbed out of his car and looked around in awe. He was seeing the estate for the first time. Tom had jumped into the middle of the project with Rick when he hired on a year ago. He was thoroughly familiar with all the details of the estate and would make a wonderful project assistant for Caroline. Each man closed up his vehicle and converged at the hatch of Caroline's Jeep. Bundled in their winter coats with hats, gloves and boots, they both looked ready to work.

"Good afternoon, gentlemen. Are you ready to shoot with me?" Caroline greeted the men as they approached.

Tom chuckled. He had run into Caroline on more than

one occasion at the actual shooting range. They both carried a concealed firearm and took time regularly to practice at the range. She was a good shot and provided more than adequate competition and encouragement to improve his aim. They occasionally arranged a mock break-in scenario at each other's homes for practice; with dry fire rounds, of course.

"Wouldn't it be fun to set up a mock break-in here?" Tom grinned at her.

"Oh, wow, it sure would. All those doorways and looping rooms and corridors - that would be such a challenge. Of course, it would probably be more fun as a game of laser tag." Caroline just beamed as the scene played out in her imagination.

Caleb looked at them, confused.

Holding out a large pink smoothie, Tom offered a chivalrous bow of his head and said, "For you, my lady."

"Why, thank you sir." She received her late lunch and took a long sip. "Oh, that's so good, and I'm so hungry. Not even the cold will bother me." She took another sip. "Okay, I've got a plan. Since we don't have too much afternoon light, I'm going to start with the exterior. That's why I parked so far back. We'll get a beautiful shot of the pristine, untrampled snow covered grounds."

Taking a piece of paper out of her folder, she finished, "While I drink my smoothie and figure out my shot, would you pull out the items needed for the 'Exterior Shoot'?"

She handed Tom the list and strolled to the front of her vehicle. Caleb looked over Tom's shoulder to peruse the list. Looking up, both men spied the inside of her Jeep. With the seats down to extend her storage capacity, the back was full, and well packed. All of her gear was labeled with large white letters facing them: BIG TRIPOD; SMALL TRIPOD; LONG LENSES; CAMERA A; CAMERA B; BIG UMBRELLA; etc. The simplicity was brilliant.

Their gaze scanning the list, they found the section heading "Exterior Shoot" and the items listed underneath. While the two men identified and claimed gear, Caroline picked her way through the deep snow to find the spot to set her tripod to begin her shoot.

With willing hands and attitudes, and a very comprehensive list of needs, the three worked seamlessly throughout the afternoon to accomplish the task of photographing the large estate. Much care was taken to highlight the overall scene as well as pay specific attention to architectural elements throughout. Her list was so detailed, little instruction was needed. They simply moved from one task and location to the next.

Caroline had worked one other shoot with Tom, so he had a pretty good idea of what to expect. However the estate shoot would be a first for Caleb. He proved to be a quick learner with good common sense – an eager and competent assistant; accommodating and helpful. Rick would be pleased with Caroline's report.

After finalizing the last shot they completed the cleanup portion of the list. With the snow outside, they had left their boots at the door on a rug Caroline had for just that purpose and shuffled through the home in their stocking feet. That kept the floors clean and made some of the cleanup a little easier. Finally, the three packed all the gear and re-loaded Caroline's Jeep.

"Gentlemen, thank you so much for all of your help today. I had fun." Caroline beamed a smile at both men. "Caleb, did you have any idea that a photo shoot, moving furniture and lugging gear would be a part of your architectural career?"

Caleb let out a low chuckle. "No, ma'am, I did not. But I'm glad for the opportunity and the experience. I've learned quite a bit this afternoon. Thank you for letting me be a part of this project. It's been a fun day."

Caroline smiled. Turning to Tom, she said, "Next time we do the other kind of shooting. Okay? Oh, and just to confirm, we're cancelling our mock break-in this month, right?"

Answering her with a serious countenance he said,

"Yes. This is not the time for mock-anything in that regard. I was planning on visiting the range this weekend sometime." His voice now a little hopeful, he asked, "Maybe we'll run into each other?"

Caroline said, "Oh, no can do. We're pretty full up this weekend." She pulled out her phone to look at the time. "Wow! It's five-thirty. You guys were awesome today. I never could've finished this quickly without you. Now, I don't know about you, but I'm tired and hungry and ready to go home."

Tom perked up. "I do have some dinner plans tonight, so I'll just skedaddle. See you tomorrow, Miss Atherton?"

"See you tomorrow, Tom." Caroline did not think she would ever get used to all of Rick's employees calling her by her last name. It seemed so formal. But it was his rule, "a respectful precedence" he called it, and she no longer argued the point.

Closing her hatch, she turned to make her own leave. Caleb stepped forward looking a little uncertain. "Miss Atherton? May I ask? What do you do now? With all those photos, I mean."

Caroline pulled on her gloves and ear muffs. In the twilight of the evening, the temperatures had plummeted. "Well, I load them onto my computer and scroll through all of them. There is a lot of personal taste and discretion in this part of the task. I have to know what my client is looking for first. The better I know my client and the project, the easier it is for me to sort and par down the collection of photos."

She pulled her coat closed and buttoned it. She continued, clarifying. "Ultimately, I look at all the photos to find the best ones. Whether it's angle, lighting, composition or content, I look at each photo and debate the merits of each on several different criteria. I may do a little tweaking and touching up here and there to get things right. It's the tedious part of the job. I usually delete more than half of what I shoot."

Caleb was listening intently. "You sure do take a lot of photos," he said.

Caroline shifted her feet in the snow. She grinned at his comment. "Once I'm satisfied that I have a fully comprehensive body of work, I'll bring the photos to my client to look over and we'll work together to make final decisions. If something isn't quite right, we may arrange additional shoot time or even start over."

Caleb's eyes opened wide. "You mean you might have to come out and do this again?" he asked, incredulous.

"No, not this project. Mr. Stratford is one client I know quite well, and we've done this many times. But, I have had clients that aren't happy with the first shoot."

"Wow," he said, shaking his head.

"Once all the decisions are made, I will send or deliver the photos in the format agreed upon and wrap up the project." She smiled at Caleb. "You're lucky; you got to help with the hands-on part of this one."

Caleb nodded with a smile. He was trying to process all that she had said. "I've never really worked with pictures or photography in any way, so that all sounds fascinating."

He thought for a moment, a sort of recognition crossed his face, and his eyes sparkled. "Wait. All those large prints in the lobby and throughout the office – those are all yours, aren't they?"

Smiling, Caroline nodded. "Well, mine <u>and</u> Mr. Stratford's."

"Wow. You really do excellent work. I can't image how you chose such perfect prints. Again, fascinating."

Caroline looked at Caleb to judge his intent. Deciding that he was being earnest, she offered, "I'll be sorting through everything tomorrow morning before I bring things to the office in the afternoon. Would you be interested in shadowing me while I work?"

Delight filled his whole face. "Could I? Really? Oh, if I can get the okay from Mr. Stratford I would absolutely love that. Thank you."

Caroline smiled. "Well, I'll plan to get started around eight-thirty in the morning. I'll put in a good word for you with the boss, and if you get the okay, just follow the path around my house to the studio in the back. For now, I need to head home. Either way, I'll see you tomorrow."

Caleb turned and practically skipped to his car.

Caroline was pleased to see his enthusiasm was real. *One more thing to tell Rick.* She drove home with a contented smile. *Time for an evening with my two favorite men.*

CHAPTER 10

Jackson exited the back door of the house and was standing on the sidewalk beside the driveway when Caroline shut off her engine. He stepped forward to open her door.

"Welcome home. Did everything go well?"

"Thank you. Yes, it did. Tom and Caleb were great assistants. I couldn't have hoped for it to go any better. How about you?"

Caroline and Jackson each shared a little of their day while the two of them unloaded her Jeep and put away all her gear. If Jackson had not been there to help, Caroline was not sure she had the energy or discipline for the task.

"Oh, Jackson, thank you so much. I can't tell you what a blessing you have just been to me." She smiled a tired smile at him.

"My pleasure, sis. Does anything come in the house?" he asked as he put his hand on the door knob, preparing to leave.

"Just me and my purse. Otherwise, everything else

stays here." She turned off the lights, set the alarm, locked the door and shut things up for the night. "Tonight is Bible Study night with my two favorite guys. Lead on."

"I haven't been home long myself. Just enough time to drop my gear and change clothes when I heard you pull in," Jackson said as they entered the house through the back door. "I ..." he paused at the sound of Christmas music and the aroma of Chinese food wafting through the house. "Hey, Rick's here with dinner. I'm starved." He kicked off his boots and headed for the dining room.

"You go ahead, I'll be right there." Caroline called after him, stepping out of her boots. She put her purse down and sat on the stool Rick had claimed the night before during their talk. That seemed like such a long time ago. Yet, she had not had much time to reflect on anything. Suddenly, she felt weary and tired and a little overwhelmed, all mixed with butterflies and anticipation.

Looking around at the kitchen she remembered that that was where her day had started, and she had an unfinished project. And Ricky AND Jackson were waiting for her in the next room. And it was the first time for the three of them together since everything had changed. And…

"Oh, Lord, I need a little help here tonight. I don't know what this is supposed to look like between us now. I'm not sure how to act. All I really want to do right now is lay

my head down and take a nap. How do I do this, Lord? Help me."

As she came to the end of her short plea, her eyes closed, she felt arms wrap around her shoulders and a kiss on the side of her head. "Hey there, Sunshine," whispered in her ear, along with a sigh. "Oh, it feels good to wrap my arms around you."

Caroline leaned her head back on Rick's shoulder, her eyes never opening. She covered his hands with hers and smiled. She sighed. *OK, Lord. I think I can do this.*

"Hmm, that's a nice way to be greeted," Caroline responded softly. "You made good time. How'd things go on-site?"

"Fine." Rick said. "Things weren't nearly as complicated as they sounded on the phone. By the time I got there I'd had time to collect my own thoughts and perspective. Thank you for your wisdom by the way. They'd misplaced a page of the plans and were in a panic. It was an easy enough fix. Not sure why I needed to actually drive out there, but that's the day God had for me. How'd the shoot go at the estate?"

She smiled, eyes still closed, trying to drink in the moment. "Fantastic. Your helpful elves were amazing and we made excellent time on that long list of photos. The place looks spectacular; it's a gorgeous design. I'm looking forward to going through the photos in the morning."

Rick asked, "How'd Caleb do? He looked a little confused when I left. I didn't have time to brief him like I should." *Can I just hold her all night? This is so nice.*

Caroline didn't even hesitate. "He was great – attentive, quick learner, easily followed instructions. We weren't long into the shoot and he was anticipating my needs. Honestly, with their work ethic and our detailed list, most of our conversation was 'next, a little left, higher, hold it there'; we just moved along like a well-oiled machine."

Rick was a little envious of the two men. *They got to spend the whole afternoon with her.* "Oh, I wish I could've been there," he sighed, "but I'm glad it went so well."

Caroline squeezed his arms. "Honestly, I'm not sure I would have been nearly as focused if you were there. Having my handsome boyfriend on-site is not the same as my brother-slash-client. Maybe that's why God had you at the construction site today instead." She grinned over her shoulder at him.

"Hmm, boyfriend. I like the sound of that." He squeezed her tighter and smiled. "Okay, I'll concede. And I'll be content to see the photos when you bring them to the office."

"I'll work on them in the morning and bring them by after lunch some time. Does your afternoon allow for that?"

she asked.

Rick thought for a moment. Mentally he rearranged a new client meeting. "I can make that happen, yes."

Caroline added, "You know, after we finished up, Caleb was interested in what came next in the project process. If he gets the okay from his boss, he'd like to shadow me in the morning."

Rick loosened his grip and looked around at Caroline. "Really?" he queried.

Caroline looked at him, her eyes brighter than she felt, and smiled. "Mm hmm. What do you think his chances are?"

Tightening up his embrace, he rested his head against hers. Softly he said, "Well, seeing how his boss has a real soft spot for the photographer, I'm thinking it's a done deal."

Caroline giggled and the two settled back into a quiet embrace.

* * * * *

It had been several minutes since Rick entered the kitchen to retrieve Caroline. Jackson walked in quietly to see what the holdup was. The sight of the two of them made him pause, and smile. *Yea, it's going to work out just fine. Just like it should be.* He stood and watched for just a moment longer. Finally, not wanting to startle them, he quietly cleared his throat and said, "Hey, you two, dinner's getting cold. Let's eat."

They did not startle or jump. Rather, they slowly opened their eyes and took a breath. Rick gave Caroline's shoulders a gentle squeeze and unwrapped himself. Giving her a soft nudge, she stood and turned. She smiled at him, ducked her head, and walked around the far side of the island, toward the dining room passed Jackson.

Jackson watched her pass, looked at Rick and shrugged his shoulders. Rick just shook his head. "Let's eat," said Rick. And they followed Caroline to the table set up with their dinner in the dining room.

Sitting down, both men put out their hands and Caroline instinctively placed hers in each of theirs. They had shared so many meals together, it was just what they did. What was new was Rick's thumb gently rubbing the side of Caroline's hand, giving her hand a gentle squeeze and kissing her knuckles before releasing his grip. Caroline blushed; it felt so intimate.

Dinner started out quiet. Was it awkward silence or a sign that everyone was tired and hungry? Not really knowing the answer was making everyone a little uncomfortable. Rick finally broke the silence. "Okay, I'm just going to assume we're all tired and hungry and that's why it's so quiet. So, that being said, Jackson, how'd things go the past two days at work? You had quite a few meetings."

With the proverbial ice broken, the three finally loosened up and enjoyed their meal and conversation. Each took a turn sharing about the events of the last few days. It was good to reconnect as a family.

After cleaning up their dinner they all claimed their favorite seats in the living room. They picked up their Bibles to begin their study time. Lifting her Bible, Caroline discovered a single white rose tucked between the pages. She opened the book to retrieve her gift and a demure smile illuminated her face. She noticed a new highlight on the page. It was Song of Songs 2:1-2 *"I am a rose of Sharon, a lily of the valleys. Like a lily among thorns is my darling among the maidens."*

"Oh, Ricky, thank you." She lifted the rose to breathe in the sweet fragrance.

"You, <u>my darling</u>, are very welcome." Her smile was all the thanks he needed. *Wow, she's beautiful!*

Jackson watched their little exchange. Rick had always done special little things for Caroline. However, he couldn't recall ever thinking of him as a romantic when it came to women. His actions toward Caroline had always been different – he'd always treated her like a rare and special jewel. He had seen it more the past year, now more clearly than ever. *You really have been leading them to this, Lord, haven't You? Wow, a real God moment right before my eyes. Cool!*

Caroline reluctantly set aside her rose and took one more look at the highlighted verse before she turned the pages to the New Testament. "Okay, I believe we're on Ephesians chapter four and it's my turn to read. Jackson, would you start us off with prayer?"

"Me? Thanks, sis." Taking a moment to focus his thoughts, the room was once more quiet. "Dear Lord, we thank you so much for the time we have here to share in Your word together…"

The next hour was spent reading, discussing, debating, encouraging, sharing and praying. Their time together never failed to bring them closer to each other and to the Lord. As they closed their books, they sat in companionable silence for a short time.

CHAPTER 11

Caroline picked up her rose and excused herself, taking the stairs to her room. A delicate vase stood empty on her dresser. She filled it with water and slipped her rose inside. Sitting on her bed she hugged her knees and stared, and thought. A battle was threatening to overtake her from within – a growing desire for the intimacy within a romantic relationship, her commitment to a pure heart and life to honor the Lord and her conflicting apprehension of Rick's attention.

I've witnessed him persuade, flirt with, seduce and use so many women in the past. Am I just another conquest? Could he really be content to pursue a chaste courtship with me? With all of his experiences and possibilities all around him, what could he really want with me?

Nothing had happened to particularly instigate those questions or feelings during the evening, but they had been picking away at her off and on all day. That battle, however, was not new, it had been brewing in the background for many months as she tried to ignore her changing feelings for Rick. She sat and repeated the questions in her mind before a knock at her door jolted her from her contemplation.

Jackson poked his head in the door. "Rick was wondering if you still wanted to do some staining?"

Shaking off the foreboding feeling, she took a last look at her rose, climbed off her bed and said, "Yes, I hated walking away half-finished this afternoon. A little accountability to finish would be a good thing. Are you going to stain with us?"

As they descended the stairs, Jackson answered. "Well, I have a few cabinet pieces all ready to assemble in the garage. I was kind of hoping to get to those tonight. Unless I need to fill a chaperone role tonight, in which case there is plenty of space for all of us to stain cabinets." He breathed out a heavy sigh. "See, this is the weird part that I'm not sure how to handle."

Rick overheard the last part of the conversation as they entered the living room. "Yeah, I know. This is new territory that affects all of us. Caroline? How do you want to handle this tonight?"

Caroline did a double take at Rick. While she was in her room he had changed into a red long-sleeved t-shirt and jeans. He looked ready to work. *Wow, he looks good.* She wanted to allow her thoughts and her eyes to linger, but both men watched her, waiting for an answer and some direction.

She shifted her thoughts to the task at hand. "Well, we've worked on projects, alone, together for years. We are full-fledged adults, and I do have a gun strapped to my hip at all times." She tried to sound playful, but she was actually feeling weary. "And since I desperately want this kitchen finished sometime before the next decade, I say we put on our work hats and get to work. Jackson, if you want to get cabinets put together, we will be fine in here staining. Rick? Remember – gun, on my hip. No touching!"

Rick smiled a very alluring smile. "My girlfriend's packin' heat. Is that sexy or what!?!" With roving eyes he looked hungrily at Caroline and uttered a low growl.

Caroline shifted her weight and just stared blankly at Rick.

Jackson grunted. "Probably not a great endorsement for your self-control, Rick. Sheesh! Maybe I should stay inside."

With his hands up in surrender, Rick laughed. "Alright, alright, I'll behave." His right hand up in a pledge salute, Rick looked dead ahead and continued in a staccato voice. "I promise to keep my hands to myself and focus on my task of staining cabinets. I promise that there will be no inappropriate physical contact. And I will refrain from any spontaneous waltzing around the kitchen until we are appropriately chaperoned." He put his hand down and looked at Caroline.

Caroline couldn't decide if she was amused or insulted.

Rick stepped close to her, took her hand and said in a more serious voice, "I promise I'm not mocking, Caroline. Just trying to find a balance and still have fun with my two favorite people." He shifted his weight and added with a cock of his head, "And it is pretty sexy that you carry a gun. I've said that from the beginning. Be encouraged, not offended."

Rick saw a cloud move swiftly across her expression as she snidely quipped to herself, *You probably look at everything as sexy.* Quickly she stuffed her thought aside.

She looked from Rick to Jackson and back. Smiling, she squared her shoulders and reclaimed some perspective. She said, "I've always liked waltzing around the kitchen with you. So, Jackson, don't stay out there the whole time, please."

"Got it. Scheduled chaperone breaks for spontaneous kitchen waltzing. I'll be here. Now, I'm off to build cabinets." Jackson grabbed his tool belt that he had left on the floor in the corner the previous night and headed out the door.

Caroline walked over to the cabinets. "Jackson set these lower cabinets last night, so they got their first coat of stain this morning. When you called I was working on the second coat for the upper cabinets. I got to here." She pointed to her spot. "I'll pick up where I left off, you start on that end and we'll work our way toward each other."

"Sounds like what we've been doing all along – working our way toward each other." He smiled at her and stepped over to the staining supplies to get started.

* * * * *

They all made quick work of their projects, stopping only for a brief break to waltz around the kitchen, just like they had planned. They cleaned up for the night as the grandfather clock chimed out eleven-thirty. When it was late at night and the house was quiet, Caroline always thought the great old clock sounded like a soothing melody as it protectively stood sentinel over the inhabitants of the house.

"Man, I'm beat." Rick collapsed on the couch.

"Do you still have some appropriate work clothes in the closet? Why don't you just crash here. It's late and it's been snowing for the last hour," Jackson offered.

Rick mentally thought about the guest room closet. He had always kept part of his wardrobe at their house; business and casual. He had been crashing on the couch, floor or guest room bed for years. He was encouraged as he remembered refreshing his stash in the closet a week or so ago. "Well, yea, I do. Caroline?"

"I'd rather you stay here than tempt the slick roads," she said with concern. "Besides, isn't it brother's breakfast tomorrow?"

Rick knew she would be concerned about the slick roads, and he understood why. It also filled him with a warm sense of belonging when she showed her care for his wellbeing. "Why, yes it is. Alright, it's settled. I'm in for the night. Anyone up for a movie and popcorn?" *I just don't want to say good night to her, yet.*

While Rick called out movie titles from the on-line catalogue, Jackson started a fire in the fireplace and Caroline popped some popcorn and gathered up blankets.

Agreeing on a fun Christmas comedy, they dimmed the lights and all snuggled under blankets on the couch. Twenty minutes into the movie, all three were sound asleep.

At some point through the night, Jackson woke up to shift positions. Looking over at his sister, he found her curled up next to Rick, sound asleep, his arm protectively around her. Although they looked peaceful, he got up to shake Rick.

"Rick. Wake up brother. Rick." Quietly, Jackson managed to rouse Rick without disturbing Caroline. "Hey, you need to move to the other couch or the floor, brother."

Groggily, Rick half opened his eyes. "What? Why?"

Looking down at Caroline, he understood. Gently he lifted her off his shoulder and guided her down on the couch. He tucked her blanket snugly around her and placed a kiss on her forehead before grabbing a blanket for himself and hit the floor. He was out in seconds.

Jackson sprawled out on the other couch and the house was once more in a state of tranquil slumber.

CHAPTER 12

The old grandfather clock boldly and rhythmically chimed out six o'clock signaling the start of a new day. The sleeping inhabitants of the home slowly roused from their slumber, stretching and twisting in their makeshift beds.

Caroline shifted to her side and rubbed her eyes, clearing her vision. Once her eyes focused she saw Rick smiling up at her - from the floor. *That's not how the night started,* she thought and smiled. *He moved for me.*

"Morning, Sunshine. You know, if you don't throw anything at me, I'll tell you that you are the best sight to wake up to."

"And if I do throw something at you?" snickered Caroline.

Rick chuckled. "Well, then I won't tell you."

She ran her fingers through her hair and stretched again. "Well, in all honesty, it's kind of nice starting my day with you." She looked at the movement to her side. "I like starting my day with you, too, Jackson," and she flashed him a charming smile.

Jackson stood and grumbled over his shoulder, "Yeah, yeah, I've heard it all before. I'm going to get breakfast started." He yawned as he scratched his head and shuffled through the dining room to the kitchen. Caroline and Rick just laughed.

"Oh, not enough sleep. Maybe a shower will help." Caroline sat up and tried in vain to stretch out the kinks of a short night on a couch.

It took every ounce of restraint for Rick to remain on the floor. He sat on his hands to encourage some self-control. His mind, however, was not exactly cooperating as he drank in the vision before him. *Wake up, Richard! Wake up!*

Caroline gathered up her blanket and asked, "Would one of you make up a plate for me? I'll have my breakfast and quiet time in the studio. That way I'll be out of your hair for brothers' breakfast and I'll be ready to start on those photos."

"Will do." Rick said, still seated on the floor as he watched her. Calling after her, he said, "It really was nice waking up with you, so to speak."

Sarcastically, in a low voice, she muttered, "I'm sure you've said that plenty in the past." And she finished her ascent of the stairs.

"What?" He said. *Surely she didn't just...* But the

implication struck a wound. He shook his head. Once he was sure Caroline was out of ear shot, he hollered into the kitchen, "Jackson, save me from myself! Your sister is going to be the death of me!"

* * * * *

Caroline was curled up in her prayer corner when her studio door chimed. "Caroline?" Rick called.

"Back here," she said as she lowered her prayer shawl, closed her Bible and set it to the side.

It smells like Christmas in here. Rick walked through the studio and peeked his head into her corner. He smiled at the sight of her leaned up against a bevy of pillows with her prayer shawl wrapped around her shoulders. *What a sight – a beautiful woman engrossed in her relationship with the Lord. Yea, it really doesn't get any better than that.*

Caroline had wanted a special prayer corner that she could retreat to whenever she felt the need. It was just a small space carved out in, literally, a corner. Not much bigger than the size of a twin mattress, that is exactly what made the base of her little alcove. The mattress, however, was set up more like a couch than a bed, filled with oversized pillows and throw blankets. A couple of low shelves hung on the wall for her diffuser and oils, a small lamp, a box of tissues and her devotion books and Bible. Clear Christmas lights hung from the ceiling all year, along with swags of sheer fabric.

"I want everything about this little space to say peace and tranquility," she told her father and Rick as they worked on redesigning the oversized shed several years ago.

It was exactly the oasis she hoped it would be. Hours of devotions, prayer and tears had been spent in that little corner.

Rick took a knee just inside the opening. "Sorry to disturb you, but I wanted to touch base with you before I leave and you got too involved in your projects for the day."

She smiled up at him. "It's no bother. I was just praying for you, actually." She looked at his pants resting on the ground. "Careful, you might end up with glitter all over you from Wednesday's shoot. I haven't had time to clean the floor."

"Oh, I think I can handle a little glitter. Besides, I'd take a shower in the stuff if it meant spending more time with you." He flashed her a sparkling smile.

Dismissively, she threw out, "So that's how you sweet talk the ladies, huh?" *It's just a flirtatious come-on.*

Ouch. Rick frowned. "No sweet talk, and no other ladies. Just tellin' you the truth." Trying to regain a little enthusiasm, he continued. "Anyway, Caleb has orders to help you however you need. Today, he is your intern for as long as you need. I love that you're doing this and he has the chance to see this side of the work. Thank you."

"It's my pleasure. I'm glad he can see the whole project through. I really appreciated his interest in the rest of the job. Thank you for letting him help me." She sounded more like herself that time.

"You're welcome. Okay, I'm out of here. I get to start on some new plans today. Time to go earn my keep." He started to rise and stopped. "I'd sure like to crawl in there and give you a kiss good-bye."

Caroline hugged her knees close to her chest and hid her face behind her arms.

Not surprised, but a little disappointed, he said "I know. I'll see you this afternoon?"

At the sight of her nod, he rose and disappeared as quickly as he had appeared.

* * * * *

Caroline had been busy at her desk for the past half hour. She'd hoped to make some progress on sorting the engagement photos before starting on the estate. Caleb arrived just before eight-thirty.

"What a charming studio, Miss Atherton. And what a treat to be in your own back yard." Caleb looked around as he walked through with a sense of awe.

She turned to greet him. "Thank you. I can't imagine working in a big building or in the city. I'm very thankful to work right here at home. My parents were so supportive. They converted this into a studio for me as a gift and investment in my future." She smiled as she thought of her parents. Returning her attention to Caleb, she motioned toward the chair next to her. "Are you ready to get to work?"

"Yes, ma'am. Do you need anything before we jump in?" Caleb shed his suit jacket and placed it on the back of the chair.

"Just a fresh pair of eyes and ears to hear as we walk through the process." She switched screens on her new 27" monitor to reveal the first exterior shot of the estate.

Caleb took his seat and the tedious task of sorting, choosing and tweaking photos began. They worked all through the morning, stopping only for a brief, early lunch. The project wrapped up a little before one-thirty. Caroline sent Caleb off to the office with a message to Rick that she would be in around two-thirty, after she ran a few errands.

* * * * *

Rick hoped to take care of a couple more phone calls before Caroline arrived, but he wanted to ensure she was not kept outside to wait. Although he knew Caroline would walk in on her own as always, he was not sure Janice, the relatively new office assistant, would treat Caroline the way she deserved without a brief reminder.

He stepped out of his office to instruct Janice to let Caroline come right on in when she arrived and he would call for Marjory and Caleb when they were ready. Although she smiled and assured him that she would, as soon as Rick walked back into his office, Janice scowled and shook with disdain.

Janice had been hired by Rick four months ago to fill the growing need for administrative help. A single woman in her early thirties, she was a little too flirtatious and suggestive in her dealings with the men in the office and overly relaxed in her work duties. She had set her sights on the owner of the firm early on and did not like Caroline. She continually dismissed the heeding of the Office Manager, Marjory, and incorrectly imagined herself in too prominent a position in the firm, and Rick's affection.

It could not have been ten minutes after Rick's instructions before Caroline walked in. She always felt a humble sense of pride walking in those doors. She was greeted by poster sized, framed prints of her photos of Rick's realized and completed designs. *He's so talented,* she thought. She was glad she had been there from the beginning to capture it all on 'film'. She smiled and sighed.

There was a couple seated in the waiting area whom she greeted before walking to the inner office. Most of the staff was in the inner office ensconced in one project or another. Caleb and Tom leaned over a table looking at some plans. Janice filed some paperwork at her desk. Marjory and Anne entered from the hallway discussing a file.

Marjory had been with Rick from the very beginning. She was a total God-send and Rick could not have been more thankful for or blessed by her. Her gift of administration complemented Rick's work ethic and architectural talents. She had been married to her husband for over twenty years and had three kids. She had become a rock to anchor the office as more employees came on board. Rick had developed a level of confidence in her judgement and abilities, rivaled only by those of Caroline.

Anne was the first architect Rick hired two years ago. She had an established reputation and, at five years his senior, brought a level of experience and history to balance out Rick's vision. He was grateful for her positive, no-nonsense approach to life. Hired shortly after the loss of her husband to cancer, she and her teenaged son had quickly found a soft spot in Rick's heart as the newest members of his small firm.

"Good afternoon everyone." Caroline smiled as she

greeted the staff. “Are you all ready for tonight?” She enjoyed a few minutes of conversation before looking at the clock. As Anne stepped to the lobby to welcome her clients, Caroline said, “Well, don’t let me keep you any longer from your work, and I am headed in to do the same. I’ll see you all this evening.”

Caroline had always had a standing invitation to enter Rick’s office unannounced, whether she was expected or not. She tossed her coat over her arm, picked up her bags and made her way toward his door. That was when Janice stepped into her path.

With thinly vailed haughtiness in her voice, and in a volume louder than an appropriate level of discretion would dictate, Janice attempted to undermine the instructions of her boss. “I’m sorry, Miss Atherton, but Mr. Stratford is in the middle of some very important phone calls. I can’t let you disturb him.”

“I assure you, Janice, Mr. Stratford will not be bothered by my arrival. Please step aside.” She could feel the tension in the air. All activity in the office ceased. All eyes and ears focused on the scene that erupted before them.

CHAPTER 13

Finishing up his last phone call, Rick thought he heard Caroline's voice outside his office door. He stepped around his desk to make his way toward the door when it suddenly flew open. Rick's smile faded immediately upon seeing the look of fire on Caroline's face.

She stormed into his office and closed the door behind her securely and with a little too much force.

Well, this can't be good, he thought.

She thrust her coat and bags in the overstuffed chair by the door.

Caroline pointed a finger at Rick and flashed a look at him he couldn't quite put a label on. "You might remember during the vetting of resumes before you interviewed her I said I had a feeling. I couldn't explain it and later you said she interviewed the best and you were pleased with her qualifications."

Caroline's tone was more than tense as she walked across the floor. "Well, I don't know how she behaves during a regular day here at the office, but I just had a most unpleasant confrontation with Janice."

Rick just stared at her, listening. He'd had to thwart a few inappropriate advances from Janice over the past couple of weeks and Marjory had spoken ill of her work performance. Even Tom had expressed concerns on several fronts about her behavior. He had spoken with his mentor, Mr. Enderly, and even his lawyer, but not Caroline. He knew she would be concerned. Seeing her now, he could not recall ever seeing her so, what? Angry? Embarrassed? *I don't know what to call this.* He waited quietly to hear what she would say next, his own emotions beginning to stir in a jumbled mix.

Standing in the middle of his office she now pointed to the door. "She just physically blocked my entrance to your office and confronted me like an impudent thirteen year old, insinuating herself in a <u>most</u> inappropriate way, showing absolutely no discretion or propriety. She even had the audacity to inquire 'who I thought I was', informing me with crude insinuations dripping from her every word that she could take care of whatever I might have for you." Taking a breath, she stormed to the picture window.

Rick attempted to calm his own rising anger. Cautiously, he inquired, "And how did you handle this?"

Reflecting on what came next, Caroline's fury

proceeded to escalate. She turned to face Rick, put her hands on her hips and purposefully punctuated each word. "I informed her that 'who I am' is the mistress of this firm and I would not suffer her impudence much longer. I informed her that wisdom would dictate that she remove herself from my path and not cross it again."

The look on Rick's face changed from concern and anger to veiled amusement right before her eyes. His look made her realize just what she had done. "Oh, Ricky, I think I may have overstepped here. I'm sorry. Oh, dear, I…"

"You haven't overstepped anything, Caroline. You are the mistress of this firm. I have always considered you as such - maybe not by specific word," he said smiling, "but certainly by definition - and I expect my staff to treat you as such. I believe you have felt the autonomy that you have here."

He stepped closer to her, invaded all appropriate boundaries, slipped his hand onto her waist and said in a low sultry voice, "And if I have my way you'll soon be an equal owner of this firm, sharing the name above the door, eliminating any question or confusion about 'who you are.'"

Stepping back to lean against his desk, his voice held a hint of mirth as he continued. "I just wish I could've seen the look on her face as you asserted your authority."

Rick recovered a tone of seriousness that matched the

circumstances before he asked, "Did anyone else witness this?"

It took Caroline a moment to recover from the heat of his hand on her waist and the rush his words gave her. Haltingly she began, "Well, Anne was just greeting a client to escort them to the conference room when Janice confronted me so rudely. She looked at me a little concerned. I nodded for her to continue and she shut the door behind her."

Her boiling anger settled into a high simmer as she mentally visualized the inner office during the encounter. "Tom and Caleb discreetly sneaked out, but I'm pretty sure they hovered in the hallway to listen. Marjory stood resolutely to the side over my shoulder."

Rick crossed his arms, nodded, and snickered, although there was nothing amusing about what his employee had done. "What exactly did she say to you?"

Caroline blushed with anger. "I won't repeat her words. You'll have to talk with one of the others for that, they all heard her." Shaking off the negativity, she continued. "I could see before I even opened my mouth that Janice registered something as a result of everyone else's actions, but she foolishly held her ground." She breathed out a sigh. "Have you had any problems with her?"

"There have been a few… situations that I've had to

traverse recently and I've been seeking advice on that front. And I have had some of the others approach me about her. I assure you, this will be addressed before the day's end. I will NOT tolerate such behavior."

She smiled a weary smile. She could see that he was on her side completely. "Thanks, Ricky."

He snickered again and his eyes sparkled. "Man, I love your spunk. And your strength." Holding out his arms, he asked, "Permission to hug the fierce and fearless 'mistress of the firm'?"

She stepped into his waiting arms and she relaxed her body into his. "Yes, please." She closed her eyes with a sigh. "And thank you for not making me feel foolish."

Rick said softly to her, "I will always champion you, Caroline. Always."

They stood in a quiet embrace for a few moments before the warning bells slowly began to sound in Rick's brain. He released her and shifted his position to create a more appropriate distance between them. "Well, are you ready to get to the real reason you came by today."

"Yes," she said. She rolled her shoulders and stretched her neck before striding across the floor to her tossed bags. She called over her shoulder, "If you want to call in Marjory and Caleb, we can go over the photos. I think we got some good shots yesterday."

While Caroline straightened her coat and bags and fished out her flash drive, Rick picked up his phone and dialed Marjory's extension. "Hi Marjory. We're ready to go over the photos from the estate shoot. Would you grab whatever you need and ask Caleb to join us? Thank you. And set the phones on auto answer." *I don't want Janice talking with any clients,* he thought as he hung up the phone.

After he finished his call Caroline pulled a small bag from her belongings in the chair. Looking at Rick she said, "I had a few errands to run before I came here. While I was out I saw this and I couldn't resist. I thought it would look good on your desk."

Walking toward his desk Caroline handed the bag to Rick.

He couldn't tell from her expression what she had done as he took the bag from her. Looking inside, Rick let out a hearty chuckle as he lifted out a Little Miss Sunshine figurine. The shiny yellow ball with her hair in pigtails smiled up at him brightly. "I love it, Caroline! It's perfect!"

He reached out a hand to caress her cheek before he placed his gift next to the photo on his desk. "I think she'll look perfect right there," he said.

Caroline giggled as Rick walked around the desk to pull a chair to the other side for her. Next to him is where she always sat for the photo review task, but that day it felt a little proprietary. Not that Caleb or Marjory needed the visual, but he thought Caroline might after what had just happened with Janice. *Or am I the one who needs it today? Hmm.*

By the time the other two joined them, the photos were loaded and projected on the retractable screen in front of the wall so everyone would have a good view. Caroline took control of the mouse and the direction of the meeting.

An hour later all decisions had been made for the publication submission. They had chosen a handful of shots for the website and even decided on a beautiful exterior shot for the wall of projects. A couple of detailed architectural close-up shots were also chosen for the 'war room' wall, aka the conference room, and several more for the project book.

Caroline usually took meticulous notes during such a meeting. Working with Rick was a treat. Marjory was an excellent administrator, so Caroline would collect a copy of her notes before leaving.

Marjory and Caleb stood to leave. "Miss Atherton, I'll have those notes ready for you when you leave. Is there anything else you need, Mr. Stratford?" Marjory inquired.

Rick answered kindly, "No. Thank you, both of you." With a slight edge to his voice, Rick added, "Marjory, when Caroline and I are finished I need to see you and Tom."

"Yes, sir." With a nod, they exited the office leaving

the door ajar.

Caroline closed down the program and ejected her flash drive. Now that they were alone, she inquired, "Did I get the architectural features the way you wanted? I'm really not sure on some of them."

"Your eye for architectural lines and structure has improved so much, Caroline. And your work is beautiful. I couldn't ask for a more perfect composition in your photos. I think this is your best collection yet. And when you lose yourself in the artistry and beauty of a subject, your work is flawless. The photo we picked for the wall is absolutely breathtaking. Makes me even more sorry I missed this experience with you."

She looked at him, a little embarrassed. "Wow, Ricky. Thank you. Such high praise."

"And it's all deserved." He looked at the clock on the wall. "Looks like we should wrap up here. I have a few things to do before we close up shop and it is party night. I was hoping to let everyone go home a little early and time is ticking away quickly." He lifted her coat from the chair and eased her into it. Resting his hands on her shoulders, he whispered in her ear, "And I'll see you at five-fifteen. I don't think I've ever looked more forward to an office party."

Trailing his fingers down her arm, he took her hand in his and led her through the doorway. Tom was leaning against the hallway entrance. Marjory was standing just a few steps outside Rick's door, holding out the copies of her notes for Caroline. Caleb was filling the copier. Anne was waiting nearby with a file in her hand. Janice was sitting sternly behind her desk, hidden behind Marjory. All eyes watched the two silently.

With a smile and a thank you, they collected the notes from Marjory as they passed. Rick opened the exterior door for Caroline, lifted her hand to his lips for a tender kiss, and she was gone.

He stood quietly at the door and watched her safely enter her Jeep Grand Cherokee before turning to face his office. He paused and surveyed the artwork adorning the wall. *It's all her work, and mine. Beautifully blended. Wow. That's almost prophetic.* He squared his shoulders and turned toward the inner office. Without a word, Marjory and Tom followed him into his office and the door was shut.

CHAPTER 14

Upstairs in her room, Caroline put the finishing touches on her hair and makeup. She had spent hours looking up ideas on Pinterest before she finally decided on a style. She had been experimenting all month in preparation for tonight's party. The final result pleased her greatly.

She stopped often to look at the white rose Rick had slipped into her Bible the night before. *I wonder if he's always been this romantic with women. Or is this just part of his routine?* She shook her head and refocused on the rose. *'Like a lily among thorns is my darling among the maidens.' And he called me his darling.*

She sighed. "Okay, Caroline," she said to herself in the mirror as she focused on her reflection, "get it together and enjoy a beautiful evening on the water with your man." She giggled and turned to finish dressing.

Rick and Jackson were standing in the living room chatting. At the sound of Caroline on the stairs, they looked her way. Both men's eyes locked on her, mouths agape and, in unison, breathed out, “Wow!”

Caroline halted three steps from the bottom and smiled at them. Her long dark hair was twisted up in a loose French knot with delicate tendrils cascading down one side and over her shoulder. Her skin shimmered and looked flawless. She wore a flowing pant suit of rich ivory velvet and satin. The soft crushed velvet pants draped in thick folds and flared at the base; the long-sleeved top boasted a delicate and modest princess cut Queen Ann neckline and long tailored waist.

Jackson nudged Rick forward with his elbow. With a stutter step, he approached the stairs, his eyes never leaving her.

Caroline watched him watching her. His look sent a thrill through her. She also noticed just how dashing he looked as well. Rick no longer wore his jeans and sweater from earlier. He was dressed in a charcoal grey, three-piece suit with a midnight blue linen shirt and black snowflake and penguin tie. *Wow! He looks so good. And I love his sense of humor in his ties. A perfect reflection of his personality.*

Mesmerized, Rick lifted his hand to escort her down the remaining steps. “You look like an angel, Caroline. You’ve taken my breath away.” He stood close to her, her hand still in his.

From off to the side, Jackson piped in. “I know you’re

my sister, Caroline, but you look absolutely beautiful. Gotta say, I'm a little jealous of Rick right now."

"Aw, you guys are going to make me blush. Thank you. It's not too much, is it?"

"No!" Both men answered emphatically.

Caroline covered her giggle with her free hand and looked away. Recovering herself, she said, "I was hoping to finish the look with Mom's pearl earrings, but I couldn't find them. I feel a little incomplete."

"Well, then it's a good thing I'm here to complete you." With a satisfied look, Rick lifted a black velvet-covered box from his pocket. He opened it to reveal a pair of pearl and diamond teardrop earrings set in white gold. "Will these do?"

Caroline caught her breath. She looked deep into Rick's eyes for a long moment. "They're beautiful, Ricky. You shouldn't have." Receiving the box in her hand, she smiled and she stepped over to the mirror on the wall in the foyer to put on the earrings.

Rick said, "I saw them in a shop window on the square and they just had your name on them. Mom's earrings are safe. I asked Jackson to move them, just in case you went looking for them for tonight."

"You boys are sneaky," Caroline said. With her newly adorned earrings, she turned to face him. "How do they look?"

"You," said Rick, "look beautiful."

"They're such an extravagant gift, Ricky. You really shouldn't have."

He stepped closer to her, tenderly touched his hand to her cheek, and looked full into her eyes. With deep sincerity, he said, "You are the extravagant gift, Sunshine. Everything else is just chaff swirling in the wind."

He had never spoken to her quite like that before. The level of intimacy in his look, his touch and his voice was intoxicating. He leaned down to place a kiss on her forehead. *Wow,* was all she could think. She didn't quite know how to respond.

Rick stepped to her side, his arm now around her waist, and asked Jackson, "What do you think, ole boy? Are we fit for the high seas?"

Jackson crossed his arms, leaned against the doorway and looked long and hard at the couple before him. They looked perfect together. How could he not have seen it earlier? He supposed because it was not time yet. Now, however, the time was right. Straightening, he said, "Yea, you'll do."

As Rick helped Caroline on with her coat, Jackson quipped in a deep, gruff voice, "Now, son, you make sure she's home by ten-thirty now, you hear?"

They all laughed. Rick jovially replied, “I can’t promise ten-thirty, but I will bring her home safely. See you later, brother.”

Jackson kissed his sister on the cheek before they made their way into the night.

* * * * *

That year’s company Christmas party would be aboard a private yacht. It was owned and captained by a college buddy of Rick’s who ran a dinner/party cruise service. Rick ran into him one day while visiting a construction site near the marina. They talked and Rick thought it would be perfect for his office party. Even with the buddy discount, though, it was a little lavish, but it had been such a good year for business, Rick wanted to do something special for everyone. Not only would they enjoy a private four hour dinner cruise around the lake with their dates, but each employee would receive an envelope at evening’s end containing a bonus.

Rick and Caroline arrived early to meet the crew, take a private tour of the yacht and go over last minute details. The yacht was an 80 foot Explorer that the captain had remodeled, converting it for his dinner cruise. The main salon was surrounded by windows which allowed for a beautiful three hundred and sixty degree view of the water or shoreline while the diners enjoyed their meal protected from the weather. Tables were set up in an intimate cluster in the aft section by the double doors leading to the aft deck. A modest dance floor had been portioned out between the tables and the upper salon with white lights hanging from above.

The upper salon had been expanded and housed the bar and galley where the crew worked and spent any down time during the cruise. The captain, however, spent his time in the fully enclosed flybridge up above. The lower deck accommodated three spacious state rooms and crew quarters to sleep four.

After their quick tour, Rick and Caroline stood next to the captain to greet the guests as they boarded. Once aboard, the activities director would show each guest to the main salon. There they could have their portrait taken and order a drink while they waited for the rest of the festivities. With Caroline's help, Rick had hired a photographer to capture the evening for everyone and provide a special memento.

Caleb and his date were the first to arrive, followed closely by Marjory and her husband. Ten minutes later, Tom and his girlfriend scurried up the ramp. After Rick greeted Anne and her son, he turned and said, "That's a full house Captain. We are good to shove off."

"Very well. Enjoy your cruise. I'll touch base with you before you disembark." He shook Rick's hand and tipped his hat to Caroline. "Ma'am."

Caroline looked quizzically at Rick. "Forgive me for not being disappointed but aren't we missing someone?"

"Nope." He entwined her arm through his. "My entire staff is aboard." With a stunned look on her face, Rick escorted her toward the bow so they could be alone for a few minutes as they drifted from port. "Close your mouth, dear."

CHAPTER 15

Side by side, the two stood alone on deck to watch the lights fade on the shore as the yacht drifted away from the dock. All around her seemed to sparkle – the water, the stars, the lights. It was a lovely sight. The moon would not rise until later in the evening, so the clear, dark night sky twinkled with star light. But it was more than a little chilly, and breezy. Caroline was glad she still wore her coat and Rick wrapped his arms around her from behind for a little extra warmth.

Caroline hesitated before asking, "Will you tell me what happened?" She didn't really want to spoil the moment or the night by bringing up the subject, but she also wanted to know.

Rick took a long breath before responding. "Well, I didn't want to spoil the evening by talking about it, but we'll just get it out of the way and leave it behind us. Okay?"

"Okay." Caroline was more than a little curious.

"Well," he began, "you know I called Marjory and

Tom into my office after you left."

"Yes," she said.

"They told me everything that happened." His voice was tense as he recalled the conversation. He looked out at the water; the muscles in his jaw tightening. He turned her to face him and said, "Caroline, I am so sorry that you had to endure that. I'm appalled by her behavior." He took another breath and looked at the sky. "Short story even shorter, I terminated her immediately."

Caroline thought for a moment. Seeing how tense Rick was, she said, "I don't imagine that went over very well?"

Rick shook his head and let out a huff. "Uh, to say she took it poorly would be an understatement. She used language that made <u>me</u> blush. Honestly, I was more angry than anything to think that she would treat you in such a manner." He looked down at her. Although there was mirth in his voice, she could tell he was sincere in his words. "It's a true testimony to your character, Caroline, that you didn't deck her." He cupped her cheek in his hand and gazed into her eyes. "You amaze me every day, Sunshine. Know that I will always put you first, I will always support you, and I <u>will</u> defend you."

Caroline took his hand in hers and placed a tender kiss on his palm. "You are an amazing man, Ricky. Thank you."

Inside the main salon Rick's staff and guests mingled and chatted. Although they were thoroughly enjoying the opulence of their surroundings, their conversation was more focused on the tender and intimate moment they witnessed out on deck.

Rick and Caroline's relationship had always baffled his staff. However none of them was close enough to either of the two to fully inquire. So, they watched, and silently speculated. They knew there was a unique friendship between them, but it was always evident that it wasn't romantic. And their business relationship was rock solid. They had, however noticed something change over the past year. Watching their exchange through the window, on top of the events earlier in the day at the office, everyone hoped they were right in what they expected was happening.

In the dropping temperatures of the night air, Rick and Caroline turned once again to look out at the water for a few minutes longer. Rick's arms were wrapped protectively and warmly around her. Reluctantly, Rick leaned against her and asked, "Well, are you ready to play hostess?"

"I guess so." She looked over her shoulder at him. "This is so nice out here, just the two of us, I kind of hate to walk away."

"I know what you mean. But, we're in charge of this

party; at least for a little while. And I'm sure we've neglected our duties long enough. Besides, there is a dance floor in there that I fully intend to employ later – with you."

Unwrapping himself from her, he held out his arm. Their arms linked once more, they walked the length of the yacht to the aft deck and entered the dining salon. His staff and guests were all mingling, drinks in hand, chatting about the elegance of the yacht and the lovely night, and what a handsome couple the boss and 'mistress of the firm' were turning into. Instrumental Christmas music played in the background.

Rick and Caroline handed their coats to the activities director and attended to their guests. Now that the cruise was underway, out on the open water of the lake, each couple was seated at their own private table. Rick stood and gently tapped a spoon to his glass to get everyone's attention. He gave a speech to welcome his staff and thank everyone for all their hard work throughout the year. He singled out each of his employees, based on tenure, beginning with his newest hire. He thoughtfully offered words of specific thanks, encouragement and praise to each, complete with personal anecdotes. Then he led them in an extended grace.

From the very beginning, Caroline had been Rick's date for the year end event and the two planned much of it together. Their greatest desire was to show Christ's love in a unique way during that time of celebration of His birth. Rick knew how much each one served his firm and their clients. The Christmas party was his chance to serve them, if only in some small way. He hoped and prayed that his genuine appreciation was felt by his employees. He and Caroline had decided that they would serve at least some portion of their evening meal themselves. That night, on the yacht, would be no different.

The crew knew of the change. Once grace had been said, Rick shook out of his suit jacket and draped it over the back of his chair. He held out Caroline's chair as she rose and they made their way to the galley steps. They joined the activity and comradery in the upper salon as each donned a full length apron.

"Everything in here smells wonderful." Rick smiled at the crew as he helped Caroline tie on her apron.

"Will you be taking the appetizers and the salads out together?" asked the head waitress.

"That's sound like a great plan. Thank you."

With plates in hand they gingerly descended the three steps to the lower dining salon and began to serve the twice baked potato appetizers and Caesar salads to each table together. It was a simple gesture, but they hoped it made a strong and positive impression.

After four return trips to the galley steps, and placing

their own plates at their table, they returned the aprons and thanked the crew for all their work. Rick followed Caroline to their own private table and they began their meal.

* * * * *

The dessert was set out buffet style at the bar for the guests to serve themselves at his or her leisure. The soft Christmas music had been exchanged for dance music by the bartender who did double duty as DJ. The younger set had already taken to the dance floor when a country song came on and a line-dance started.

Up sprang Caroline's head. "Ooh, I know this one." Looking at Rick, she asked, "Do you mind?" She knew Rick didn't know but one country line dance, and the Tush Push was not it.

"Don't be silly. Go. Dance." he said.

With a youthful grin, Caroline trotted out to the dance floor to join the others.

Rick sat back in his seat and watched her with full admiration. Her face was lit up in a smile so full of life, and she moved with such ease through the steps. For a brief moment, life seemed to move in slow motion. *God, she's amazing. Thank you.*

As he sat, taking in the scene before him, Rick

marveled at where the Lord had led him and how richly He had provided for him. *And if everything disappeared and all that remained was Caroline, I'd still be the richest man in the world.*

"She sure looks beautiful tonight." The voice was that of Marjory's husband, Walter.

"She sure does," Rick said dreamily. Breaking his focus, he looked up to register who'd spoken. He motioned to the empty seat and said, "Please, join me, Walter."

"I sense something different about you two tonight. Are we <u>finally</u> going to hear a special announcement?" Since Marjory had been with Rick from the very beginning of opening his firm, she and her husband were the only guests to be served dinner by Rick and Caroline that first year, at a dinner party at Rick's townhome. Walter and Rick had struck up a casual friendship over the years.

Rick grinned and once again turned his attention to the dance floor. "Not just yet, but we have started that journey." He looked back at Walter. With a twinkle in his eye he said, "But don't let that get around, now."

At that moment, the music changed to a slow song. "Ah, now that's what I've been waiting for." Rick pushed his chair back and walked around his table. "If you'll excuse me, Walter, it's my turn on the dance floor with a very beautiful lady," and he quickly sailed across the room.

Rick met Caroline at the edge of the dance floor, made a small bow, took her in his arms and the two swept around the dance floor in an elegant waltz. With the same magic as at the steak house, their surroundings faded away and they had eyes only for each other. Gazing into each other's eyes, believing in the changes upon them, the hope and the promises, they were living in the moment, in the song, in each other's hearts.

Little did they know that they were the only ones on the dance floor. All the others watched from the fringe as they enjoyed the scene before them. The love that was blossoming between their boss and the 'mistress of the firm' was more than evident to all. Even the crew and the captain looked on from the shadows while the photographer discreetly captured the magic of the scene.

Rick masterfully led Caroline. They had danced together so often that neither had to concentrate on the steps. Caroline easily yielded to his direction and felt completely secure in his embrace. They had not danced with such vigor in a while, though. Time and space had been scarce. That night, they abandoned themselves to the moment. Exhilarating!

As the music faded they slowed their pace. One last spin, arms held at length, they stopped. He kissed her hand and the room around them returned, once again, into focus.

Their guests were all clapping. Shyly, but with a little flair, Caroline curtsied and Rick took a bow. YMCA began to play which brought the others to converge on the dance floor.

Breathlessly, Caroline said, "Oh, my, that was fun. Thank you, Ricky." *And magical; I feel like I'm in a fairytale.*

"It's always my pleasure to dance with you, Sunshine. But that really was fun." Catching his own breath, he breathed out, "Water?"

"Yes, please." And the two made their way to the bar.

* * * * *

They all danced a little more. They all laughed a little more. They enjoyed a little dessert and a little more conversation. The mood was light and festive. Everyone had such a nice time.

Late into the evening, Caroline looked out the window and noticed the full moon as it began its rise on the horizon. "Oh, Rick, look!" she said with awe as she delicately pointed out the window.

Rick took her hand in his and quickly ushered her once more to the aft deck so they could enjoy the beauty of the moonrise in, what he hoped would remain, private. They huddled together at the rail, having rushed into the cold night air.

Discreetly, one of the crew arrived with their coats and quickly and quietly disappeared. As Rick moved to drape his own coat over the rail before he helped Caroline on with hers, Rick caught a slight movement up high out of the corner of his eye. Looking up he noticed the captain looking down at them from outside his perch on the flybridge. He tipped his hat to Rick before he turned back to his duties and the warmth of his enclosure. Rick made a slight nod with a smile.

They stood with their shoulders touching. Their breath hung in the air, a testament to how cold the night air had become. Looking out over the shimmering water the big, bright moon climbed higher into the sky. It was a true 'Joe versus the Volcano' moon, looking larger than life as it appeared to hover above the water.

Rick glanced over at Caroline. "This has really been a magical night, Caroline. Unlike any other Christmas party, or any other… anything, really. Thank you for sharing it with me."

She slipped her arm through his as she sidled up closer to him. "It has been a lovely night. Who knew when we first started planning this how it would be." Caroline leaned her head onto Rick's shoulder.

"I think I've been a little selfish with my time

tonight," Rick said.

"Something tells me the staff didn't mind," Caroline said softly.

Rick chuckled.

They stood silently staring at the moon. The sound of the festivities filtered out from the salon. As the yacht continued to glide through the water, Rick turned. Gazing down at Caroline, he whispered, "I have never enjoyed someone's company more than I have enjoyed being with you tonight."

The yacht was slowing through the strait, headed for the marina.

Like so many of Rick's more intimate comments, once again insecurity and doubt were ignited within Caroline. The internal response and all the unfamiliar feelings continued to throw Caroline for such a loop, she once again acted out uncharacteristically. She straightened and glanced up at Rick before stepping away from the rail. Almost to herself she quipped, "Oh, I doubt that," as she walked back into the dining salon.

Her words struck deep. There was no mistaking what he'd heard that time. Rick looked after her quizzically. *Why would she doubt me?* He tried to shrug it off. He did not want anything to cloud the evening. *It's been such a perfect evening. Where did that come from? I know she's struggling with something. It'll work out in time. But I hope it's soon, Lord.*

He paused for one last look at the moon, said a quick prayer for the rest of the night, and walked into the dining salon to take care of the last order of business before seeing his guests off for the night.

* * * * *

With all of the guests gone, Rick and Caroline enjoyed a simple night cap with the Captain up in the enclosed flybridge. The rest of the crew cleaned up below and the photographer gathered together his gear.

"Well, Rick, I've hosted a lot of events in the six years I've been doing this and I gotta tell you, two things. First, your people are awesome. No gossip, no drunkenness, no rudeness. They all actually like each other and enjoy spending time together. Not all company parties are like that."

Rick beamed. "Thanks, Cap. They really are a good group of people. I'm a blessed man to work with them."

Cap continued. "And, second, you two. Not only did everyone here hold you two in the highest regard and affection, something I'm not sure I've ever seen in this situation, but you two can dance!"

Rick and Caroline chuckled. "Thanks. Caroline and I have been dancing together for years. And she's a natural. I've always been grateful to be her partner." Rick squeezed Caroline's hand.

The Captain looked from Rick to Caroline and back again. "Wait a minute. All those dance competitions in college," he looked at Caroline, "that was you?"

Caroline smiled and nodded her head. "Guilty as charged," she said.

Returning his focus to Rick, Cap whistled and said, "Man, I'm sorry we gave you so much grief. After what I saw tonight I now know why you endured so much razzing."

Rick cast an adoring look at Caroline. "Some things are worth putting up with a little teasing."

Caroline smiled up at him. *He never even hinted that he took flak from his friends. I'm sure glad he stuck with it.*

"Well, it was more than just a little teasing and you know it, but I can see why you didn't quit." Suddenly, the Captain had a thought. "Look, I'm staying on board tonight. We've got a brunch cruise at ten-thirty. Why don't I unlock a couple of the rooms below and you can enjoy the rest of the night on the water as my guests. There are clean robes and fresh supplies in the bathrooms."

Rick did not even need to look at Caroline or take a moment to consider before responding. "Wow, Cap, that's a very generous offer. Thank you. But, a raincheck maybe?"

"Absolutely. And hey, you're still on the VIP list. One day I hope you take advantage of it. I still can't believe this is the first time you've been aboard."

Caroline listened with interest. *Rick said 'generous offer' not 'tempting offer'. He's being true to his word. And he's never been aboard? I wonder why not?*

"Well, you crazy kids, if you'll excuse me, I have some things to go over with the crew before I call it a night. Stay aboard as long as you like. The night watchman will lock up the gate after he sees you leave. It's been a pleasure." Cap once again shook Rick's hand and tipped his hat to Caroline before he escorted the two down the stairwell to the galley and continued to the crew quarters.

As they stood in the galley, Rick looked at Caroline. Hopeful, he asked, "Are you up for one last dance?"

Looking up at him, her eyes sparkled. She nodded.

He looked at the bartender standing silently off to the side, giving the countertop one last wipe down. "How about you, sir? Are you willing to stick around for one last dance?"

He thought for a moment, looked at the non-existent watch on his wrist and replied in his low baritone voice, "Well, sir, I'm not quite as light on my feet as the lady, but if you insist…"

The three laughed. As Rick led Caroline down the

three steps to the lower salon and to the dance floor, the bartender turned on one last slow song.

CHAPTER 16

Buried under covers, her mind began to awaken as the magic of the previous night flooded her memory. Caroline rolled onto her back, put her hands behind her head, and smiled a dreamy smile.

She thought back over the week and marveled that it had only been three nights since she and Rick had their first official date and serious talk. It had been so natural to cross that friendship bridge as they transitioned into their courtship.

And yet, Caroline had experienced a fiercely growing battle within. Her feelings and thoughts were a conflicted and jumbled mess. She was excited to see Rick and spend time with him. She marveled at how safe and cared for he made her feel. The magnetism between them was undeniable and alluring. And yet, doubts about Rick's intentions had crept into her thoughts more and more. As she explored the ideas and realities of intimacy within a romantic relationship, she became increasingly confused as to what was appropriate in the eyes of the Lord and her own comfort level.

She tried to think about the last three days with clarity. Caroline had to admit that Rick had only been attentive, supportive, championing and respectful. He had held true to his promises about decorum. *So why do I harbor such doubts?* she thought as she lay there.

Sitting up, she repositioned her pillows against the headboard. Leaning over to her side table she picked up her small travel Bible. *I don't know where to go, Lord.*

She grabbed her iPod and opened her Bible Concordance app. She looked up 'marriage' and 'wife'. For the next two hours she read, scribbled notes, and challenged and argued with the Lord over all the passages she could find. First Corinthians 7 seemed to stick in her thoughts more than others.

She glanced once more at the words, "Do not deprive each other except by mutual consent and for a time, so that you may devote yourselves to prayer." *Life got pretty busy these past few days. Maybe I need a little more prayer on this topic.*

As she set her things aside, there was a knock at the door.

"Caroline, are you in there?"

"I'm here, big brother. Come on in," she called out to the door.

As Jackson walked in, he spied her Bible open on her bed. That sight alleviated any concerns he had that something might be wrong. "I'm just checking on you. You don't usually lazy around this late when we have plans."

She looked at the clock. Eleven forty-five. "Oh my word! I totally didn't realize. I guess I got caught up reading. I'm sorry."

He chuckled. "No apologies. As long as you're alright."

"I am." She gave him a guilty grin.

"Last night?" He inquired.

Her eyes sparkled and she said, "Very good."

"I want to hear all about it, but right now, come down stairs. I want to show you something." He looked almost giddy.

Caroline slipped into her slippers and threw her robe around her as she followed Jackson down the stairs and into the kitchen.

Jackson stood at the entryway and beamed. As she walked passed him, she was in awe at the sight before her. "Jackson, how did you do all this?"

All the remaining cabinets and the pantry were completely installed. Even the holes for the hardware were drilled. The countertops had been placed and secured. The windows were beautifully trimmed out, and the crown molding surrounded the room.

Jackson was pleased he could surprise his sister. "I was working away shortly after you guys left when Mr. Enderly popped in for a chat. It's been a while since we'd had a visit so we just started talking while I continued to work. The next thing I know he's holding things, we're measuring and cutting. After a time we stood back and looked at - this." He held up his hands at the room. "What do you think?"

"Oh, Jackson, it's beautiful." Tears threatened to fall from her eyes.

Jackson said, "It felt so good to get to this point. It was kind of like working with Dad. I've missed him a lot, working on this. Sometimes I wonder if that's why it's gone so slow."

"Dad would be proud of the work you've done here, Jackson." Caroline looked compassionately at her brother.

"The work <u>we've</u> done. And, hey, I did learn from the best. He might not be here, but there's a lot of him in this room."

Caroline walked to her brother and gave him a hug. His arm around her, her head rested on his shoulder, the two stood and looked at their kitchen; every thought of their parents.

The sound of Jackson's phone invaded their quiet

reverie.

"Hey, brother, what's up?" He paused briefly. "Well, I'm ready to walk out the door, but someone is still in her PJs." He shot a sassy look at Caroline. "Well, you might think that, but I just see a sleepy head… Yea, I've already got it in the truck… I'll tell her. See you then."

"Uh oh, you'll tell me what?" Caroline asked.

"I quote, 'shake your tail feathers; the birds are waiting.' Also, pack what you want for tomorrow, the weather is supposed to get a little dicey tonight so I'd rather just stay put."

"Got it." Caroline nodded.

"Now, dear sister of mine, go shake." And Jackson waved his hand toward the stairs.

Today was Winter Solstice.

* * * * *

The sight of Rick's place as they pulled up the lane always took Caroline's breath away. His home was a beautiful ranch estate surrounded by twenty acres of wooded land at the edge of town. It included three oversized bedrooms, a master suite and a guest suite, 5 full and 2 half bathrooms, 4 fireplaces, a formal living room and a great room, a dining room, a gourmet kitchen, plus a breakfast nook, laundry room, mud room and an extended three car garage. The basement was partially storage with the rest wired as an entertainment mecca. Beautiful natural wood connected the house throughout and it boasted generous twelve foot ceilings. Windows lined the exterior walls allowing as much natural light and beauty to enter the home as possible.

Six years ago Rick designed the home for a local prominent business man and his wife. He had been given an enormous amount of latitude, so he let his own dreams and desires pour out all over the design. The client fell in love with the designs and the home was built. Three years ago the man died. Over the course of the next year, his widow ran into serious financial trouble and the property went back to the bank. Diligently he watched the activity; once it came up for auction, Rick was able to acquire the property significantly below its market value. He always said that the privilege of owning it himself felt like an undeserved gift.

The grounds were an outdoor enthusiast's paradise. It was where Caroline felt most at home. She had spent hours exploring the woods and creeks, ditches and overlooks, with her camera bag in tow. Several of her photographs were either framed or would be printed and framed later to adorn the walls of the home. Rick had always been generous with his support and encouragement of Caroline's talent and he wanted his home to be filled with items of a personal nature to reflect who he was, and that meant the outdoors.

Rick still sometimes felt overwhelmed, coming from his humble townhome to such an extravagant estate. Much of the home was still closed up and undecorated since he didn't need that much space for just himself – even though Caroline and Jackson used it as a second home.

In preparation for the move-in, Rick had spent a good deal of time with Mom getting the kitchen fully stocked. They had so much fun shopping and planning together and Rick had learned a number of new kitchen skills. Everywhere they looked – in cabinets, on the stove, at the linens – she was there.

Over the course of the first year, Rick, Caroline and Jackson had worked on furnishing and decorating the great room, as well as the master and guest suites and one bedroom. It would take time, but they were in no rush. It was a fun project to work on together.

* * * * *

As Jackson circled the drive, they could see the canopy and tables set up near a roaring fire as Rick piled on more logs. Jackson pulled his truck straight into the garage. While Jackson walked out to greet Rick, Caroline went into the house. She took her bags to her suite and hung up her clothes.

It wasn't long before Caroline made her way toward the canopy in the yard. Rick had set things up close to the humble beginnings of their bird sanctuary. Rick greeted her and lifted her off the ground into his arms.

"Ah, there's my Sunshine. You know, whether in satin and pearls or denim and fleece, you're beautiful." On that cold winter day Caroline was wearing her flannel lined jeans, a mossy green henley under a moss and lavender flannel button shirt under an extra-long chocolate colored fleece hooded jacket, crowned with a fleece hat; her feet clad in snug winter boots. She was ready for her day outdoors.

With her arms around his neck, her feet dangled above the snow. Caroline smiled at Rick. "Aw, shucks, Ricky. You're awfully handsome yourself." Rick was dressed in jeans with a navy blue turtleneck under a navy blue cable knit sweater under his dark brown field coat and work boots – just the way Caroline liked him best.

Rick gently settled her on the ground and took her hand. "Come on. I have something for you." He led her to the shelter where tables were set up with all the food and supplies for their Winter Solstice fun. Mugs of hot cocoa waited for the three of them. Set up on one of the tables was a large box. As she took a sip of her cocoa, Caroline motioned questioningly toward the box.

Rick and Jackson looked at one another. Jackson motioned toward Rick, "It's your project, brother, you do the honors."

Rick took a breath before he began. "At last year's winter solstice, Dad and I started talking about making a whole colony of bird feeders and bird houses to place around our bird sanctuary here. It was a project we'd work on together throughout the year, and it was going to be a surprise."

He paused and choked up a little. "Unfortunately we never even had a chance to get started."

At the mention of her father, tears began to burn Caroline's eyes. Rick had been accepted into their family by everyone and he had been affectionately calling her parents Mom and Dad for almost as long as he had known them. She knew their loss was felt just as deeply by Rick as by herself and her brother.

"The idea nagged at the back of my mind for a while before I finally shared it with Jackson. We spent some time talking about what we wanted to do to honor that idea, and their memory. It was a challenge to sneak in the time, but over the past few months, Jackson and I made these."

Jackson lifted the box off the table. Nestled beneath were three unique bird feeders. Caroline just stared. As the guys continued to share, her tears fell unchecked down her cheeks.

Rick lifted up a feeder that looked like a house with a platform base, a roof and wrought iron details. He said, "This one is in honor of Dad. He accepted me into his home and gave me shelter from the storms of life and loved me like his own son. He set quite an example for all of us of what a home and family should look like."

He moved on to a small swinging porch chair feeder. "This one… is in honor of Mom," Rick's voice began to crack, "… who spent countless hours talking with me, sharing her wisdom and, and her love, no matter what was going on."

Unable to go on, he looked at Jackson. Jackson took the hook of the last feeder and walked around the table. It was a three-tiered pagoda style feeder. "This one represents the three of us; individuals but one unit. We've stuck together through so much, and we'll continue to do so; growing and living life together."

There were silent sniffles as the three stood in a small circle and remembered the two people they loved and missed so much. Their absence left a hole in every activity and every event. Never was it more deeply felt than at Christmas.

Caroline walked to her brother, who in turn welcomed both she and Rick in a tight family embrace.

Muffled inside the tight circle, Caroline managed to say, “Thank you guys so much. What a beautiful gift.”

Once they all dried their tears, they each picked up a bird feeder and a shepherd’s hook from against a tree and they walked to a spot that Rick had picked out to place them. Thus kicked off their annual tradition of feeding the birds on the longest night of winter.

Tears turned to laughter as they spread peanut butter on bagels and dipped them in bird seed, strung popcorn and cranberries, looped circle cereal into a string wreath, and made a whole host of food ornaments to adorn the trees in the yard for the furry and feathery wildlife.

As the solstice would dictate, the sun set early on their festivities. They had made s’mores and snacked on almost as much food as they put on the trees. The last of the fading light was used to pack up all the supplies. As darkness surrounded them, they gathered around the dwindling fire for a little warmth. It wasn’t long before the snow began to fall.

“I’ve got the last of the food,” Jackson said as he walked away and lifted the big box into his arms. “I’m headed in,” and he marched his way through the snow to the house.

Caroline gathered a basket with the last of the supplies and Rick doused the fire with snow. While they walked back slowly through the snow, Rick asked, "So, did you really like the bird feeders?"

"Oh, Ricky, they're prefect," she said. "Mom and Dad would've been so pleased. And they're perfect for the bird sanctuary we're developing over there. I love it."

He stopped in front of her and looked down into her smiling face. Her head was covered in snow, her nose and cheeks rosy pink from the cold and her eyes sparkled like stars. *I think now is the time. Why should I wait any longer to tell her?* Rick took in a deep breath, stepped a little closer to her, smiled nervously and…

"Hey you guys," Jackson yelled from the garage, "get in here and look at this storm that's moving in."

The moment lost, the two picked up their pace to the house. They shook off the snow in the garage, hung up their winter gear and padded into the house. They were greeted by the wonderful aroma of the crock pot stew Rick had put on before the festivities began. Caroline stopped only long enough to grab her house slippers and followed the guys into the great room to look at the weather forecast.

"Hmm, we might lose power tonight. Good thing the oil lamps and candles are all out." Rick thought out loud. "Let's get more wood in the wood box and bring out some extra blankets. We'll get the fire going and be ready for whatever happens. It might be another living room slumber party."

Winters could be brutal at times, but they had their routine down pat. They all scattered to their usual tasks and met back together fifteen minutes later in the kitchen. It was time for dinner.

*****

The power was knocked out about eight o'clock. Their little party didn't miss a beat, though. With all their earlier preparation, they were comfortable and warm, had plenty of munchies and were so deep into a game of Monopoly that they hardly registered when the room went dark. Caroline was the first one out, as usual. While Rick and Jackson 'fought to the death' for the nightly title of Monopoly King, Caroline crawled up on the couch and fell asleep.

CHAPTER 17

The sound of clanking dishes and the aroma of freshly brewed coffee and baking cinnamon rolls awakened Caroline's senses in the early morning hours. She pulled back her blanket and stumbled into the kitchen while she detangled her hair with a finger comb.

"Hey, she lives," came Jackson's cheerful greeting.

She yawned and said, "Good morning. How much snow did we get?" She reached her hands out for the coffee mug he offered her. *Ahh, a real mug; what a treat.*

"About a foot and a half. It was a good one." He walked over to the window. "It sure is beautiful."

She joined him at the window and sighed her agreement. "I see we have power. That's good."

Jackson nodded. "Yea, it was on when we got up. Definitely thankful for that."

Caroline asked, "Where's Ricky?"

"He's outside plowing the drive. We've been up for a little over an hour. I decided to come in and make some breakfast," Jackson said.

"And it smells good, too." Rick called out as he blew in the door. "I'm done. Whew! I tell you, I'm not sure I like the long drive in the winter. The other seasons it's great. But winter, not so much. At least I get to use a plow; can you image doing all that with a shovel? We'd never get out of here." He planted a kiss on Caroline's forehead. "Good morning, Sunshine."

"Wow, you guys have been busy. I would've helped." Caroline felt a little guilty that they'd both worked so hard while she slept.

"Nah, you looked too peaceful sleeping. I didn't want to disturb you." Rick said. "It did take some doing to keep your brother from, well, being your brother, but I succeeded in the end – just like in Monopoly." His eyes sparkled as he raised his arms in triumph and gloated over Jackson.

"Yeah, you won last night. But I will reclaim my title. Of that you can be sure!" He huffed across the kitchen to remove the biscuits and cinnamon rolls from the oven and stir the gravy.

"You know, brother, that might sound a little more fearsome if you weren't wearing an apron." He chuckled as he tread across the floor to wash his hands.

Caroline enjoyed their banter as she pulled out plates and forks. She poured Rick a cup of coffee and they all fixed their plates. After they sat down at the table in the breakfast nook, they said grace and chatted while the local newscasters informed their viewers of all the storm related news on the television.

* * * * *

It would take more than a foot or so of snow to shut down their town. The roads were a little slow, but they made it to church just fine, all three of them in Jackson's 4x4 truck.

The church leadership had decided to consolidate the two services and move the time to accommodate some clean up after the storm. That meant the church would be full. It was also the last Sunday of Advent and the children would be sharing a program during service.

Caroline, Jackson and Rick had been attending church together for many years. Their routine was simple. Rick led the way down the aisle followed by Jackson and then Caroline. Once Rick had arrived at the row where they would sit, he and Jackson stood aside to let Caroline in first. Jackson always sat next to Caroline, and Rick closed up the end of the row. That was how it always was. Until that Sunday.

Caroline had not thought anything of it. Their routine was so ingrained that she just followed in line like always. What she did not know was that Rick and Jackson had thought about it, and had discussed it. When Rick reached the row, instead of standing to the side, he entered the row and moved to the third seat, still standing. Jackson, however, did stand aside.

Caroline looked from Jackson to Rick and back. Jackson smiled at his sister, and then nodded over to Rick. Rick held out his hand to her, receiving her at his side as she shuffled in. Jackson then filled in the final seat. She was firmly established between the two strong men in her life.

When did they decide to do this? Caroline wondered. *I feel like a caged animal on display at the circus.* Inwardly she growled and bristled.

The visual representation of the change in their relationship was noted throughout the entire congregation.

As Rick leaned over to whisper in her ear, he was cut off as the music began to play and Caroline stood.

Caroline had a hard time concentrating on the service. As if her 'spider-sense' was tingling, she heard whispers and saw looks and glances all around her. Sometimes it was only a word or a name, other times phrases. Many in the congregation had taken notice of their seating-order change and were talking about it. *This is so disruptive,* was her constant thought.

By the time service ended, Caroline was beyond uncomfortable. What the service was about, exactly, she could not even begin to recall. When Rick placed his hand on her shoulder to guide her out, she stiffened. Rick felt it. She tried to maintain her composure, and discretion, as she quickly walked out into the lobby avoiding eye contact along the way. *I need to get out of here,* was all she thought.

Rick followed her with concerned eyes as he exited the row. He kindly replied to greetings as he walked but he didn't stop to chat. As he caught up with Caroline he asked, "Hey, is everything okay? I thought we'd hang around and visit for a while."

Caroline stepped close to him in an effort to keep her voice low. "The three of us rode all the way here together, in the same truck, and you didn't think to tell me about your little plan?" she hissed at him, her tone dripped with accusation.

Uh oh. "Well, when Jackson and I talked about this, we didn't think…"

"Obviously you didn't think," Caroline interjected. "Not about me anyway." The heat from her words chafed.

Rick led her over near a wall, a little more out of the way. "How did you want to handle things, Caroline?" he asked, concern and a little irritation in his voice. Her tone had made him defensive.

"I guess we won't know that, *now*, Rick, you didn't discuss it with *me*. You discussed 'us', again, with brother Jackson. The brotherly bond prevails and that is, apparently where your loyalty lies." She started to step to the side.

Rick stepped in to block her departure. "No, Caroline. We, I…"

She interrupted him again as she spat, "You set me up and put me on display like some prize." She took a breath and looked at him. Her words came out like fiery darts. "Of course, I'm sure Jackson's always known more about your relationships with women than the women." She did not let him respond as she stepped out of their corner and set her sights on the neighbor she'd spotted on the other side of the lobby.

Rick stood still, stunned. *She's right. I should've talked with her, not Jackson. But she lost the moral high ground with that biting retort. Why is she doing this?* Feeling caught between confusion, concern and irritation, Rick did not know who to talk to at that point. Pulling himself from his faraway thoughts, he was aware that someone was talking to him.

"... lunch at the deli around the corner?" The members of their singles small group had circled him, looking at him expectantly.

Rick registered their faces, but not their words. He said, "I'm sorry, what was that? Lunch?"

They repeated their plans for a group lunch at the deli and asked again if he would be joining them. Rick distractedly kept looking over at Caroline.

"Come on, Rick, let's go get some lunch." Jackson chimed in as he joined their little group.

"Um, I'm not sure..." he said slowly and his voice trailed off as he watched Caroline walk out the main door with her neighbor and across the parking lot. He looked at Jackson.

"Hey, where's Caroline? Let's go eat." Jackson looked around the lobby.

"It looks like she just headed home with your neighbor." Rick motioned toward the main parking lot. They looked out just in time to see Caroline go by in the backseat of their neighbor's car.

* * * * *

"Thanks for the ride." Caroline shut the car door and crunched her way up her front walk and around to the back door. Inside the mud room, she stamped off her feet, slipped out of her boots and hung up her purse and coat. Not particularly hungry, but still on edge from the events and conversation at church, she marched upstairs to change into some work clothes.

First I'll go shovel the walkways and driveway, then I'll tackle the kitchen.

She attacked her projects with a vengeance. Although a constant dialogue was had in her mind, nothing about it could really be called prayer. Her internal battle about Rick's past treatment of women and his current intentions toward her raged to a new height. The battle was very real, and it was gaining momentum.

She was just finishing up staining the final section of cabinets when she heard Jackson's truck pull into the driveway. *This will be interesting.* She stood poised atop the step stool when the two men walked into the room.

Rick wasn't sure how things would go when he got to the house. He and Caroline had had disagreements before, but what happened earlier was so personal, intimate. He had never done intimate before. He'd decided that part of her accusation was correct and he owed her an apology. The other snide part he hoped he was wise in deciding to let her work out on her own; and he sure hoped that was soon.

As he walked into the house, he didn't have to look very far to find Caroline. She wore stained jeans with holes in the knees and frayed cuffs and a baggy college sweatshirt with her holster peeking out the bottom. Her hair was tied up in a messy knot and her cheeks were stain streaked. She stood atop the step stool, poised with a brush in her hand as she glared at the two of them.

I really am a goner. Even mad and disheveled, I'm beguiled. Oh boy! Rick stared at her for a moment, not able to move.

"We missed you at lunch, Caroline. A little heads-up would've been nice," came Jackson's sarcastic greeting.

"Yea, it's frustrating when people make decisions that affect you without talking about it with you first, isn't it?" Her tone was just as sarcastic. Her usual kindness and understanding was nowhere to be found. And repentant? Not a concept in her brain just then.

"What?" Jackson was confused. He looked at Rick. "Did we screw something up again?"

Rick looked at Caroline and said, "We need to talk."

She hesitated before she climbed down off the stool. She set her brush aside and leaned against the counter with her arms crossed. Jackson began to excuse himself.

"No, Jackson, you'd better stay. This actually concerns all three of us. Better we all have one discussion instead of pairing off."

"Okay." Jackson leaned against the counter and the three of them made a large triangle in the kitchen.

Rick began. "First off, I am sorry, Caroline. I didn't think about how you might want to handle letting people know about the change in our relationship. I got all caught up in wanting to let the whole world know and I took for granted that you wouldn't mind." He sighed. "And talking to Jackson? I totally didn't mean to undermine you in any way."

He turned to Jackson. "I guess we didn't learn our lesson last week, because we did do it again. We talked about Caroline and made decisions about our relationship," he pointed to Caroline, "without her. Your sister called me on my loyalty earlier, and that - stung. One thing I guess we, or I, failed to consider is that I do need to make a shift in loyalty. It sounds harsh and I wouldn't have put it that way, but from Caroline's perspective, I see what she means. It was bound to happen sooner or later, and will when you fall in love, too. Because it's Caroline, I'm afraid I took some things for granted."

Rick crossed the floor to stand directly in front of Caroline. "I'm sorry, Caroline. I'm still figuring some of this out, too. Please don't ever question my loyalty, because my heart belongs to you. Will you forgive me?"

She could see the sincerity in his eyes. She didn't think he would intentionally hurt her, even though that was much of the internal battle she continued to entertain. She was still more than a little perturbed, but she nodded her head. "I forgive you," she said with a shrug.

Jackson looked on as he pondered Rick's words and tried to make sense of everything. "So, exactly what does this mean? I lose my best friend because you fell in love with my sister?" His tone was not bitter, but lost.

"No." Rick and Caroline answered in unison as they both looked at Jackson.

Rick said, "Are you kidding? I can't imagine going through life without you as my best friend. I totally need you, brother."

Caroline offered, "I don't know that I expect your relationship to change much, really. Actually, I imagine you will learn things about your sister that you probably shouldn't know about your sister because of your relationship, and guys need to talk to guys, too, I know that. But there's a line. Arranging to move Mom's earrings was one thing. Deciding to put me on display in front of the church is another."

She turned her attention once again on Rick. "Rick, if this is going to be a real relationship, you need to talk to <u>me</u>."

"I will, I promise." Since he felt that they were on the other side of the argument and peace had been restored, Rick shifted his feet, cocked his head and smirked. "Is it alright if I tell you how sexy you looked perched on that stool when I walked in?"

Caroline groaned, "Ugh, good grief!" She slumped her shoulders, hung her head and shuffled toward the living room.

Both men laughed. "I don't know, Jackson, I might have more to learn than I thought." And Rick darted out of the kitchen in pursuit of Caroline.

CHAPTER 18

They sat in the living room together, Rick close to Caroline's side, his arm around the back of the couch, as he gently caressed her neck with his fingers and twirled the loose tendrils of her hair. The tension in Caroline had never subsided; her internal battle still being fought. As they sat there so close to each other, her irritation reached the boiling point and she scooted away and shrugged off his hand.

"Please, Ricky," she chided.

Rick scooted closer to her. "Don't pull away, Caroline. If something's wrong, talk to me, but don't pull away."

Caroline ducked away from him and sprang off the couch. Just loud enough to be heard, she shot out over her shoulder, "It's not supposed to be all about sex, Rick." She set her sights on the kitchen.

He lunged off the couch, reached out to grab her arm and turned her around before she exited the room. Careful to keep his grip firm but not harsh, he held her in front of him.

He set his tone low and tried to keep his composure. “You really have to stop doing that, Caroline.”

She looked up at him, surprise and defiance flashing in her eyes. “What?”

“Throwing out some snide, digging or dismissive comment and walking away from me. And sex?” He released her arm. “Who said anything about sex? It’s not like I’m trying to throw you against the wall and rip your clothes off. I just want to be close to you.”

Defensively, Caroline held her ground. “Women have always been an object to you, a game. How do I know that’s not what this is now? I’m sure with your vast physical experience this is no big deal to you.” She threw her words at him. All the internal grumbling finally exploded.

“Women? There are no ‘women’, Caroline. There is only you!” As he realized the full meaning of her words, he looked down at her with fire in his eyes. “And you think I’m playing a game with you? Trust me, Caroline, this is no game. I really thought you knew me better than that.”

Still defensive, she retorted, “You agreed, no physical stuff. Maybe you enjoy making me uncomfortable by touching me in such a, a sensual way or being so close to me or always making some kind of sexual reference.”

Rick was through trying to deny that he was angry. He had had enough of her insinuations, her baiting and her insecurities. "Yes, the 'physical stuff' that is the gift and pleasure of the intimacy of marriage will be held at bay until then. But, Caroline, I have always hugged you, I have always kissed you on the cheek, I have always held your hand. I've always done those things with you, and I'm not going to stop, certainly not now!"

His voice strained as he tried to control his emotions. "I love being close to you, I love touching you. And, yes, I'm not ashamed to admit that I can't wait to be able to touch you more. And it isn't because of my *vast physical experience* that has me desiring you, Caroline, it's because you are 100% woman and I am 100% man and I am so completely in love with you I want to share every part of what that means – with You!"

Caroline's eyes grew wide. She had never seen Rick so angry at her. Slowly, her defensive wall began to crack. He was yelling at her. And he was not finished.

"But just because I *want* does not mean I'm going to *take*. I made you that promise and I have kept my word. More importantly, I have kept my promise to God. Not because I don't *want* to, because oh – my – heavens, Caroline, I WANT to. I've chosen this path because I want you to know, beyond the shadow of a doubt, that it is YOU I love, that it is OUR relationship that I value and that, second only to the Lord, I am committed to YOU and only YOU,

NOT the physical stuff. I respect you so completely and I have enough self-control, thanks to the Holy Spirit, to say 'no' and wait."

He inched so close to her, he could feel her breath, but his hands remained at his side. He continued with a low voice, filled with emotion and desire. "When we make love, Caroline, I want it to be making love within the sanctity of holy matrimony where we are both free to break this tie that binds us and dive, unbridled into the passion that's boiling just below the surface and express our love for one another so purely and so completely."

He backed away, his voice raised. "But we will never be able to do that if you keep holding over my head the fact that I've had sex before, keeping a record of my wrong. I may have had sex before, but I have never made love to a woman the way I want to make love with you. I have never shared myself with any woman the way I want to and have been sharing myself with you. And if you continue to measure yourself against some warped idea of what you think it was like, or they were like, you'll never be free to be yourself in a marriage relationship, with anyone."

Turning in the middle of the living room, he ran his hand through his hair. Caroline stood frozen to the floor. Rick went on. "I have worked hard to put my past behind me. The truth of the gospel has given me permission to consider myself a new creation, and that includes considering myself a born-again virgin. I haven't even thought about dating anyone since I became a Christian because I gave that whole part of my life to Him, too, and so I've waited. <u>And you know this!</u>"

He glared at her. "You've said you support me and that you're proud of me, but your actions and your attitude NOW tell me that you don't forgive me and you are judging me for all my past sins; sins God has forgiven me for and I've forgiven myself, but you're holding against me and using as stumbling blocks to our future. You don't seem to believe me when I say I've never felt any of this before or had any kind of a relationship like this. You contradict my statements, which is just like calling me a liar."

He threw up his hands, growled, and paced. His voice lowered and steady, he kept a respectful distance from her as he continued. "You need to make up your mind, Caroline. Are you going to really live this faith you have? The one of forgiveness and second chances and renewal and transformation? Because if you are, then you're going to have to accept that that is what God has already given me, and you're going to have to be willing to give it to me, too."

Rick took a small step forward, his voice filled with weariness. "And if you love me then you're going to have to trust me. If you're not willing to do that, you better reexamine this deep faith of yours because you're just deluding yourself. And I will not spend the rest of my life apologizing to YOU for my past or trying to convince you to believe in the man that I've become."

He took a breath and heard that 'still, small voice' that told him he had reached the end of his argument. If he continued, it would be a rapid descent into his anger leading him into sin. It was time to walk away. So, without another word, he marched through the house, grabbed his coat and walked out the back door. He trudged through the snow and climbed into Jackson's truck.

Caroline stood in the living room in stunned silence. Her eyes welled up with tears. But it was not because he had yelled at her, it was because he was right. His words, the pain she saw in his eyes, and the passion she heard in his voice revealed a truth that she had not seen in herself. She had become so blinded by her internal battle and the deception she entertained in her mind that she never really brought her fears to the Lord, or looked at them through the filter of His word.

Before she could take a step or have another thought, Jackson emerged from the shadow of the foyer. He leaned against the wall and looked at his sister with disappointment. He was angry with her. He had come to expect a certain attitude and perspective from her. Condemnation and intentional hurtfulness were not part of it.

He crossed his arms as he confronted her. "You know, Caroline, I've been Rick's best friend for a long time. And I've seen a lot of behavior and heard a lot of things from him. This might hurt for you to hear, but I think you need to hear it."

Jackson took a lazy step forward. "I've watch Rick pick up women at bars and party hard. I've heard all of his lines and come-ons. I've seen him totally drunk making time with a woman in a hallway, whose name he never bothered to get. I've seen him stumble into the apartment half-dressed after spending part of the night with some other no-named woman. I've seen him seduce women, use women and throw women away without a second thought."

Caroline looked away, tears streamed down her cheeks. She had known some of that and suspected the rest, in theory, but as she heard the words of confirmation, it cut deep.

Jackson continued. "I'll tell you what I've never seen him do, though. And that's romance a woman. Or love a woman. Or give any real part of himself to a woman. Heck, I've never even seen him actually date a woman. I've never seen him care so much about a woman that he would sacrifice <u>everything</u> for her. Until you."

He stared hard at his sister as he walked across the

room. “And that's because that other Rick doesn't exist anymore. He died when he gave his life to Christ. The Rick who is courting you, Caroline, pulling out all the stops to win your heart, eager and excited to see you and make you laugh and bring you joy, submitting his desires to your sensibilities - that is a God molded, Holy Spirit shaken, transformed man who loves you, and only you. There is no comparison to anything. All this - this is nothing he's ever experienced before."

Caroline continued to cry. "Stop. Please stop."

Jackson knew it was hard, but there was more. "You’re my sister, Caroline, and I love you. I've always had your back and looked out for you. I'd never let anyone hurt you. But Rick is also my brother and my best friend. And I love him and I've got his back, too. And right now, Caroline, you are wrong. You are hurting him, deeply, and you are wrong. Rick has been a lot of things in the past, but he has never been a liar, and you know it. The man you know now, and, I suspect, love, he deserves your respect, your devotion, your love and your trust."

Jackson knew he could say no more. He hoped she had heard him. The rest was up to her. With the sound of her sobs ringing in his ears, he walked through the house, grabbed his coat and walked out the back door.

Caroline stood in the living room alone. The

emptiness of the house enveloped her. But it was not a peaceful emptiness. It was a cold, hollow emptiness.

"Oh, Mom, I wish you were here" she cried aloud. But Caroline knew that, even if her mother was still alive, she could not help her with the heart of the matter. That was something she could only work through with one person – her Lord.

CHAPTER 19

Tears streamed down Caroline's cheeks. The hollow emptiness of the house enveloped her, suffocating her. The silence was deafening. She needed to escape. And she knew exactly where she needed to go. Blinded by tears, she trudged down the back hall, stepped into her boots, lifted her purse off the hook and made her way to her studio.

Caroline knew her studio well and could navigate its space easily in the dark. She lifted her prayer shawl from the hook on the wall and crawled into her special prayer corner. With a decisive click, the small light on the shelf softly illuminated her sanctuary. A few drops of a peaceful oil blend dripped into the diffuser before she turned it on. Taking a moment to let the scent envelope her, she lifted her Bible off the pillow and settled in for what would be a long night of prayer and supplication.

She replayed all the words both Rick and Jackson had said to her. She also began to review the thoughts that had been haunting her in earnest over the past week. Caroline realized that she could be proud of and forgive her brother, Ricky, and encourage him to have a new life in and for the Lord. She had witnessed it in his life. She knew it was real.

But what were her expectations for her boyfriend, Ricky? Her future husband? No, she held him to a different standard: he was supposed to be blameless and pure, kept pure for her. To accept Rick for the transformed man he was now and give herself wholly to him, to trust him with all of her love, in the most intimate ways, would be to open herself up to vulnerabilities that confirmed all of her insecurities.

"Oh, dear God, who am I, and what have I done? I have been such a hypocrite. And I have hurt the man I hold most dear. And, Lord, I have sinned, against You and against my family. Ricky was right; I have been keeping a record of his wrongs. Oh, Lord, I am so sorry; please help me to figure this all out."

Caroline knew only one approach to submitting herself to God's authority and His word. She could only rely on her earlier studies as she flipped through the pages of her Bible and read and prayed over highlighted passages. She hungered for His guidance, His compassion, His wisdom and His love. She knew the answers were there, and so she began.

She began in the book of Psalm. Caroline knew that He would hear her cry. She read fervently and prayed back the words as they related to her situation.

She read aloud the words of Psalm 91, verse four. "He will cover you with his feathers, and under his wings you will find refuge; his faithfulness will be your shield and rampart." *Thank you, Lord, for being my shield; that even in the ugly and messy parts of life, You are my refuge.*

Caroline turned the pages and stopped at Psalm 141. She read the first five verses aloud, "O Lord, I call to you; come quickly to me. Hear my voice when I call to you. May my prayer be set before you like incense; may the lifting up of my hands be like the evening sacrifice. Set a guard over my mouth, O Lord, keep watch over the door of my lips. Let not my heart be drawn to what is evil, to take part in wicked deeds with men who are evildoers; let me not eat of their delicacies." She lifted up her hands, lowered her head and prayed, *O Lord I let the enemy trick me with his lies; my words to Ricky have been spiteful and mean-spirited. Forgive me, Lord.*

She lingered over the passage and her prayer. It was several minutes before she continued to read. "Let a righteous man strike me - it is a kindness; let him rebuke me, it is oil on my head. My head will not refuse it." *You have blessed me with two strong, Godly men in my life, Lord; they have been harsh with me tonight, they have rebuked me,* her tears sprang forth afresh, *but I needed to hear it; Thank you for Your truths. Thank You for opening the eyes of my heart,*

Lord.

She turned another page. Psalm 143 caught her attention. Again she read the words of the highlighted passage aloud, "Answer me quickly, O Lord; my spirit fails. Do not hide your face from me or I will be like those who go down to the pit. Let the morning bring me word of your unfailing love, for I have put my trust in you. Show me the way I should go, for to you I lift up my soul. Rescue me from my enemies, O Lord, for I hide myself in you. Teach me to do your will, for you are my God; may your good Spirit lead me on level ground." She closed her eyes. *May Your answers come quickly, Lord. Show me, Lord, guide me in my searching tonight; rescue me beyond my unbelief and beyond my fears.*

Caroline fervently flipped the pages. A highlighted section of 2 Corinthians chapter five jumped off the page. Slowly she read, "So from now on we regard no one from a worldly point of view. Though we once regarded Christ in this way, we do so no longer. Therefore, if anyone is in Christ, he is a new creation; the old has gone, the new has come! All this is from God, who reconciled us to himself through Christ and gave us the ministry of reconciliation: that God was reconciling the world to himself in Christ, not counting men's sins against them. And he has committed to us the message of reconciliation."

And there it was; the truth of the gospel in black and white. She had allowed herself to carry a pride in her heart and ignored what she knew to be true. *Do I believe that Ricky is a new creation; made new in You, Lord? How can I not? I have witnessed his transformation for myself, in countless ways. He is NOT the man he used to be; the man I have been secretly accusing him of being. The man I have been holding against him.*

She reached over to one of the shelves and lifted up a photo frame. The frame contained a photo of Rick, Jackson and her. It was the same photo that adorned Rick's desk. Her eyes focused solely on Rick. *I know who he is now, who he's been for six years, a man after Your heart, Lord. A man whose love and embrace and commitment I can be secure in. A man who deserves more respect than I've given him this week. May You lead me in reconciliation with him?*

Completely humbled and submitted to the work of the Holy Spirit, she was able to lay her fears, her insecurities and her doubts before the Lord at the foot of the cross. She could physically feel the burden lifted. The veil that had threatened to blind the eyes of her heart was gone. All she felt in her heart at that moment was the unadulterated love and affection Ricky had shown her all week, all year. *I do trust him, Lord. And I do love him.*

Slowly she turned the pages back where she found a

bookmark she had made some time ago. It marked the passage of 1 Corinthians 13. While she studied the famous 'Love passage' one night, she wondered what it would look like to see only "Love is" statements. So, after looking up the words, she'd hand written her findings on a piece of card stock.

As she held her bookmark she read slowly, focused on each word. "Love is: Patient, Kind, Joyful, Humble, Encouraging, Polite, Selfless, Calm/Even Tempered, Forgiving, Pure, Protective."

I could put Ricky's name next to each of these traits, Lord. Will You help me to be this for him, as well?

Quietly she sat in her corner. Caroline finally felt the peace that had been missing the past several days. The words of an old hymn swelled within. *It is well, with my soul.* She sat in silence for some time and continued to pray as she sought direction from the Lord. She revisited the verses she had looked up earlier about marriage and relationship and she realigned her head and her heart to sync up with the path she so completely wanted to take with Rick.

The diffuser had long since shut off as she leaned over to turn off the soft light in the corner. She stood, hung up her prayer shawl, and exited her studio. Stepping out into the pre-dawn hour, Caroline was met with a fierce wind and more falling snow. Undaunted, she climbed into her Jeep, shifted into four-wheel drive and backed out of the driveway.

* * * * *

Her Jeep securely parked between Rick's Jeep and Jackson's truck, Caroline let herself into Rick's home. She padded across the floor in her stocking feet; she searched with listening ears. There was little evidence of life in the house. Christian music resounded throughout and firelight flickered and glowed from the great room. Otherwise, everything was still. Stopping in the doorway of the great room, her eyes alighted upon Rick, seated on the floor before the fire, his eyes closed.

"I prayed you'd come." He opened his eyes and look at her wearily.

She crawled onto the rug close beside him and looked him full in the face. Her eyes were clear; they sparkled with repentance and hope.

"I'm so sorry, Ricky. I've been such a fool and a hypocrite." From there, Caroline poured out her heart and the journey she had just taken with the Lord. She did not leave anything out. All of her insecurities, her doubts, lies she had been listening to; nothing was held back. Rick had already stripped himself bare and made himself completely vulnerable to her. It was time she did the same.

"I didn't mean to be unfair, or cruel," she sighed, "or insecure. And I certainly didn't mean to hurt you." She paused for a short breath. "I do love you, Ricky, with all of my heart, and I know the truth of the Godly man you are today. If you'll still have it, Ricky, if you'll still have me, I offer freely my respect, my devotion, my love and my trust." Hesitantly she added shyly, "All of me. Will you forgive me?"

The weariness had faded from his eyes. He'd listened intently and forced himself to keep from interrupting her. Everything he had been praying for all night sat before him, her words a soothing and healing balm to his wounded heart. He could see that the cloud of doubt was gone from her face and the barrier of fear and insecurity no longer lingered. *I don't know why I get this gift, Lord, this blessing, but I can't thank You enough.*

He sat up straight and brought his face just inches from hers. He slid his fingers through the tangled hair along her neck and rubbed his thumb softly back and forth across her cheek. He looked longingly into her eyes. "Yes, Sunshine, I forgive you." He closed his eyes briefly and took a deep breath. "I love you, Caroline Atherton. Deeply and passionately. To borrow a phrase, may you come to grasp how wide and long and high and deep is my love for you."

He did not move or take his eyes off her, but raised

his voice just a touch. “I’m going to kiss your sister now, Jackson.”

From around the corner in the kitchen came, “Okay, I’ll close my eyes.”

Caroline slid her arms around Rick. He leaned into her and their lips touched, soft and tender, then more intently. Lightning flashed through their bodies. They crossed all bounds of propriety and decorum as they indulged in a long, slow, passionate kiss.

CHAPTER 20

Reluctantly, Rick pulled back from their embrace. Those flashing red lights were blinking wildly, mixed also with horns blaring. He looked at Caroline and thought, *I wonder if my grin's as goofy as hers. I hope so.*

"I'm pretty sure that just broke the rules," Rick said unrepentantly.

Caroline's eyes sparkled and she smiled. "Well, I'm pretty sure I'm just as culpable."

"Is it safe for me to come in?" Jackson slowly oozed around the corner from the kitchen and into the great room. He reached out a hand to Caroline and helped her up.

"Jackson, thank you – for being my big brother, even when it's hard, and for being honest with me." She wrapped her arms around him.

"Ah, that's part of my job, little sister." Jackson held her back and looked from her to Rick. "Now, everything is bet-ter?"

"Bet-ter! Comtriya!" All three said at once and fell

into a round of laughter.

Rick excused himself for a moment and Caroline and Jackson sat down on the couch.

"Did you guys get any sleep?" Caroline asked.

"No. We talked for a while, we prayed. He listened to music. But mostly, he just sat quietly staring at the fire. I was just being his friend. Plus, no offense, but I didn't really want to be at the house."

"None taken," said Caroline. "Honestly, I've never felt more alone than when you both walked out. Even I walked out. I spent the whole time in my prayer corner in the studio." She hesitated. "Are you still mad at me?"

Jackson smiled a crooked smile at her. "No. I heard everything you said to Rick. I'm sorry you were struggling so much. But I'm glad you worked your way through it. I'm sorry I had to take sides; I don't want to do that again."

"Me neither." She looked up as Rick walked back into the room. He was carrying a plain brown box. "It's not Christmas, yet. What's in the box?"

Rick put the box on the coffee table and sat on the floor opposite the two. "Well," he began, "this was supposed to be for yesterday, but we never quite got to dinner, so… Caroline?" He motioned for her to open the box.

Like a little girl, she opened the top and looked in. "Oh, wow." Gingerly, she pulled out a medium sized oval galvanized tub wrapped with a Christmas tartan ribbon and filled with pine cones, pine boughs, cranberry branches and four large white pillar candles.

Rick explained, "This Christmas season has been kind of funky. What with missing the folks, your house a war zone, I mean construction zone," he dodged a flying pillow from Jackson and managed to continue, "busy schedules, et cetera; none of us pulled out any decorations, not even the Advent wreath. I've missed it more than I thought I would. I couldn't bear abandoning all the Christmas traditions we've enjoyed together."

He looked at Caroline. "And, I was hoping to create a few special Christmas memories with you this year, Caroline. I didn't want to go searching for the family Advent wreath among all the boxes and chaos, so I adapted. Yes, I admit, Pinterest is my friend."

"You made that?" Jackson raised his eyebrows; he looked stunned.

"Yes, I made it; don't sound so shocked. I'm very secure in my manhood – *and* I can tie pretty bows and squirt a mean glue gun, so watch out. Anyway, I was hoping you guys would light it with me at dinner yesterday and read some of the scriptures. Not sure what to do now."

After a brief moment of silent contemplation, Caroline walked to the fireplace and retrieved a lighter that rested on the hearth. Returning to her spot on the couch, she leaned over and lit the first candle. "The Prophesy Candle. Jesus' birth was foretold in the book of Isaiah to the Hebrews. They were given hope in the King to come."

She passed the lighter to Rick. He looked at her for a moment. With a smile and a nod, he lit the second candle. "The Love Candle. Jesus is the greatest love offering from God to His people. And Jesus' love for us - giving us a living, breathing example of the truest meaning of love."

Rick passed the lighter to Jackson. He lit the third candle. "The Shepherd's Candle. The shepherds were filled with a fear, an awe and a joy at the announcement of Christ's birth. Jesus is our shepherd, leading us on a path to righteousness and to the Father. He is our joy, even amidst the storms."

The lighter rested once more in Caroline's hand. The last candle lit, she said, "The Angel's Candle which represents peace. Jesus said, 'Peace I leave with you; my peace I give you. I do not give to you as the world gives. Do not let your hearts be troubled and do not be afraid.'"

Caroline laid the lighter on the table and reached her hands out to both men. Her hands in each, she squeezed Rick's hand. Without a word, all three bowed their heads and Rick led them in a prayer of thanks for the gift of the baby Jesus and the season to remember and celebrate with the two most important people in his life.

* * * * *

Caroline enjoyed the view of the bird sanctuary out the kitchen window as she cleaned up from breakfast. It was a rare treat to witness the wildlife at such an early hour of the morning as the first shadow of light began to dawn on the day. Two deer, a couple of bunny rabbits, several squirrels, and more birds than she could count were enjoying the buffet they had laid out for them. *It's just like I always hoped it would look.*

"Hey, Caroline? Where's your coat?" Rick called out as he made his way into the house after once more plowing the drive.

With a slightly guilty look on her face, she turned. "At home?" She smiled brightly.

"You mean to tell me you drove out here, in the freezing temperatures and snow, in the middle of the night, in just that?" He pointed to the outfit she had been wearing when he entered her kitchen after lunch yesterday.

With a little "hee hee," she answered, "Well, I slipped on my boots. Honestly, I didn't even think about it. I had something more important on my mind."

His features softened as he put his arms around her

waist. "Well, I guess I can't argue with that." His hand fumbled around the holster on her hip. He looked around her and said, "You really do wear that all the time, don't you?"

"Well, yes, that's kind of the point. Plus, it's kind of just part of getting dressed now, like wearing a belt or a necklace."

"Even out here?" He didn't want her to feel unsafe in his home. He wanted her to be fully free there.

"Ah, but I didn't start out here. It's easier to just keep it on. Besides, I don't have a lock box here to put it in, so it's safer where it is."

He nodded thoughtfully and then a sparkle gleamed in his eye. "I guess it's a good thing I think it's sexy, huh." And he squeezed her tighter.

She swiped the dishtowel in her hand at him before she rested her head on his chest. His comment did not make her stiffen, or have doubts. All she felt was giddy. *He thinks I'm sexy.* His attention and intimate statement finally settled into her as sheer love and devotion; a promise of the future, a future she was excited to discover. She sighed and said, "I'm envious of you today. You get to work from home all snug and warm in this beautiful place."

Rick's mind quickly jumped to the blueprints he'd been working on. He forced himself to return to the present. "Why jealous? You work from home all the time. And isn't that what you're getting ready to do?"

"Well, yes, but I have to leave first. You just get to grab a cup of coffee and go sit at your table."

"True, true. It is going to be a difficult day." He held her tight. "All alone in this big house I'm not sure I'll be able to concentrate on anything but that kiss," he said playfully. Her smile let him know that she would be thinking of it often through the day, too.

Jackson walked across the room and sat down at the table. "Alright, Caroline, you need to leave so I can go to work. This chaperone has stuff to do before I break for Christmas. Plus, I need a few minutes with my brother first. So, chop chop."

One last kiss for each, she confirmed their dinner and Christmas plans and then Caroline was out the door – with one of Rick's coats wrapped around her.

Rick walked Caroline to her Jeep and watched as she pulled into the street and disappeared from view before he returned to the kitchen where Jackson waited. "You'll be here for lunch?"

"Yea, I've got the afternoon off, and then through Christmas," Jackson said, "I'll pick up pizzas on the way. Will you be ready?"

Rick grinned. "I'm almost finished with the plans, so I'm chomping at the bit to get them out and on the table.

Hopefully, I can have those finished and sent to Marjory so she can print them in time. And then I'll have the boxes all out and ready when you get here."

Jackson grinned at his best friend and said, "We really can be sneaky, can't we!?"

Rick looked at him; concern clouded his expression. "This is like the earrings though, right? Good sneaky?"

Jackson patted Rick on the shoulder. "Oh, yeah, this is a good sneaky. See you later."

* * * * *

Caroline pulled into the gas station. *It's already getting busy,* she thought. *I'll just get this out of the way and go home.*

She grabbed her purse and hustled inside to pick up a couple of bottles of flavored vitamin water for later and pre-pay for her gas. She set her sights on the coolers along the back wall.

As she reached for the cooler door, there was a commotion behind her, a scream and the distinct sound of a shotgun as it chambered a round.

Oh, God, no!

CHAPTER 21

Caroline saw the people in the store scatter behind displays and huddle in corners. She quickly ducked behind an aisle and reached back for her sidearm. As she pulled it out of its holster she heard a small gasp behind her. She noticed a little girl and mom huddled close by as she looked over her shoulder. Her finger over her lips signaled them to stay quiet and then she motioned for them to move back.

A man brandishing a shotgun was yelling at the clerk behind the counter.

"Is this where you met him? Is he here now, hiding, that …"

Caroline tuned out his rant as she closed her eyes. *Okay, this is why you train. No family here will go through what we did if I can help it.* She took a deep breath. *Stop. Focus. Think.* She looked around trying to get a grasp on her surroundings. *He's yelling at someone. This sounds personal, not a robbery. Okay.* She shifted her weight to sneak a peek around the display.

She had a profile view of the man. He was pacing as he kept his eyes frantically focused on the clerk. His gun was pointed up and his finger was on the trigger.

Oh, not good. Just like she had done many times in practice, she firmly grasped her weapon, lifted her arms, her finger rested against the barrel, the safety on. *Breathe*. She lined up her shot and looked behind the intruder. *Rats*. A man and teenage boy huddled low, well off to the side but a little closer to her line of sight than she would like.

The intruder's rants seemed to escalate; he was shaking, filled with anger, and seemed confused. "I won't let you do this. I told you, you…"

Caroline listened to his continued barrage of insults and accusations. She waited until there was a break in his focus. She called on all of her strength and hoped her voice came out bold and clear. "Sir, we would really appreciate it if you put your weapon down."

The man looked around and waived the shotgun erratically. "Who said that?" he yelled.

"My name is Caroline, and I need you to know that I do have a weapon, sir." Her voice was steady and clear.

The intruder cursed at her, multiple times, and inquired if she was a cop.

"I am trained to use my firearm, sir, but I do not want to. There are children here, sir, lots of people who are now in danger and frightened. I can see that there are some things you need to say to this woman. Please, put your weapon down and we'll all hear each other much clearer."

She'd been wracking her brain to figure out how to get the man and teenager to move. She couldn't come up with anything. *They really are out of my way, but still...* she thought. Her mind raced with scenarios as she decided if she trusted her shot, her ability… and her resolve.

"She promised me. Don't you see? Why would she do this?" He turned his attention back to the clerk. "Why would you …" and he proceeded to question the woman behind the desk with jumbled agitation; his anger once again rising. The gist of the story was, she left him; he thought it was for another man. Caroline just listened and prayed for some divine wisdom.

Once she heard another chance to insert herself into the conversation, she tried again to redirect his focus. "Sir, I can't claim to know what you're feeling right now, but I can see that you're angry and hurt."

He interjected, "You bet I'm angry." His attention and his shotgun were riveted once more on the clerk. "Answer me!"

A few whimpers were heard around the store.

Okay, that was a fail. Caroline tried again, "Sir, I'm sure it's hard to think, much less speak looking at the barrel of a shotgun. Why don't you put that gun down on the floor and we can figure this out."

He threw a few choice words Caroline's direction and then continued to badger and question the clerk more. The clerk stood mutely, shaking and crying.

This isn't working. Lord, help. I need another approach. A thought came to her. "Will you tell me your name, sir?" Caroline asked in a loud voice.

"What?" The question seemed to throw him off focus a little.

"Your name, sir? Will you tell me your name? My name's Caroline." Caroline noticed a slight movement over her shoulder. The mom had her cell phone out, pointed in her direction. Caroline looked questioningly at the woman. She mouthed '9-1-1' and pointed to her ear and back at Caroline. Caroline nodded and returned her gaze to the man up front.

"What do you care what my name is?" His voice was inquisitive. Caroline knew he was sufficiently distracted as she saw his shotgun lowered to point at the floor.

This is better. "Well, I guess I like to know the people I have conversations with. My mom used to tell me when I was little, 'learn their name dear; it's much easier to make a friend when you know their name.' I miss talking with her and hearing her bits of wisdom." Caroline heard the far off sound of sirens.

"Why do you miss it?" He faced her direction fully now, his shoulders relaxed, the shotgun now cradled in his arm, his finger off the trigger. He spoke to a direction, and the small barrel of a gun, but he didn't seem to notice.

Caroline steeled herself. Not all of her story was one she enjoyed sharing. "Well, because of a situation very similar to this one, actually. A man showed up, very, very angry, at a place my parents were. He yelled and screamed and then decided he was going to shoot people. He killed my parents, and several others."

An eerie hush fell over the store as everyone waited.

The intruder was quiet for a moment. "My name's Simeon."

Caroline smiled. "Ah, a Bible name. It means something like obedient and listening."

Simeon cocked his head; a look of confusion and interest crossed his face. "It does? How do you know that?"

"Oh, I like to study the Bible and biblical history." She thought for a moment. *He looks relaxed, but don't lose your focus.* "Would you like to hear a little of the history of Simeon in the Bible?"

She could see Simeon contemplate her question. Slowly, he shrugged and answered, "Okay, sure."

"I tell you what, Simeon, why don't you put that shotgun down by the door and I'll come around and tell you about two other Simeons I've read about." *Please God, let this work.*

All eyes focused in the direction of the front desk.

Simeon hesitated. He looked at his hands. He looked in her direction.

"Simeon?" Caroline said.

He turned toward the door, took two steps forward and laid the shotgun on the floor. Slowly he turned back to face Caroline's direction and said, "Will you tell me now, Caroline?"

A collective sigh was heard throughout the store.

Caroline stepped slowly out from behind the display, her weapon lowered as she returned it to its holster. "Thank you, Simeon. I'm so glad you decided to put the shotgun down. I think we'll all breathe a little easier now." She looked around the store. "If you don't mind, everyone is going to just stay where they are while you and I talk for another minute. Okay, Simeon?"

Simeon just stood, looked at her and shrugged again.

That's good enough for me, she thought.

It was not Simeon who needed the message, it was everyone else. And it worked. She saw the shoppers stop, some even sat on the floor. What was most important was that everyone would be okay - now.

Although things seemed much calmer, Caroline's

senses were on full alert. Her hand never fully relaxed as she held it to her side, ready to reclaim her weapon if needed. Caroline smiled at Simeon as she began. "There was a Simeon in both the Old and New Testaments. Are you familiar with those, Simeon?"

Simeon shrugged, "Maybe a little."

"Good." She hoped her smile reassured him. "So, in the Old Testament, Simeon was one of the founders of the twelve tribes of Judah. He was a pretty important guy who was very serious about taking caring of his family. And in the New Testament, a man named Simeon actually held the baby Jesus a few days after he was born. He even got to say a blessing over baby Jesus and his parents."

Caroline's voice filled with wonder and joy any time she spoke of God's word. She didn't try, she just had that much passion about it. "It's said Simeon was a man who was righteous and devout. He'd had a revelation, like a dream, that he would get to see the Christ, the Savior, before he died. It was the Holy Spirit that showed him that the baby Jesus was the Savior come to Earth."

"Wow." Simeon was enthralled; captivated by her story. "Is there more?" he asked.

While Caroline shared her stories of biblical Simeons, several police cars had silently pulled into the lot. Officers stood behind car doors, and two officers cautiously approached the glass doors. Caroline made eye contact with the one in the lead. She nodded.

Caroline looked at Simeon. "Yes, Simeon, there is so much more." Her voice was filled with hope. "And I'd like to visit with you again to share it with you. But right now, Simeon, there are some other men who need to talk with you about, well, about all of this." She waved her hand toward the officers. "But it'll be alright, Simeon."

Simeon looked a little scared as the officers entered the store and addressed him, by name.

CHAPTER 22

As the officers cuffed Simeon and led him outside, the shoppers in the store came out of hiding. They surrounded Caroline as they thanked her and congratulated her. She had hardly taken the time to breathe when the little girl who had been near her tugged on her coat. Caroline knelt down and smiled. "Hi there."

"My name's Charlee. And you're brave, Caroline." The little girls eyes danced and she smiled at Caroline.

Caroline's heart melted as she gave Charlee a big hug. "Oh, thank you, Charlee, but I think you're the brave one. You and your mom. And smart, too. You stayed sooo quiet, and your mom called 9-1-1 and let them hear all that was going on. You were so brave."

Charlee smiled from ear to ear. She called out, "Thank you," before turning to her mom to ask excitedly, "Did you hear that, Mommy, I'm brave. Did you hear?" Charlee's mom smiled at Caroline and mouthed a 'thank you.'

Caroline smiled and stood. Facing her was another man who had been in the far back corner. "Was any of that true, Miss?" He looked at her skeptically.

She smiled sadly. "It was all true. The only real way to talk with anyone is with the truth."

Another woman asked, "So you're folks were part of what happened last winter?"

Caroline could only manage an "Mm hmm."

"Is that why you carry? Or did you carry before that?" came another question.

Caroline had never considered herself a spokesperson or an advocate for any political topics. All she ever really wanted to do was follow the leading of the Holy Spirit and be inside of God's will. *What do I say here?* She took a long breath and began. "Before my parents were killed I was never really concerned about guns. I didn't really know much about them. My dad taught me the basics and he and my bother enjoyed shooting and hunting now and again."

The pain of the still fresh memory stabbed at her. "But going through all that last winter, how it all happened, I came to realize that I can, I should, be more proactive about safety and awareness. So, I found a simple intro class and learned all I could. It all just flowed from there. But I don't carry so I can pull the trigger. I'd rather not pull the trigger. But if I can help make it to where no other family has to go through what my family did, than I can do that. I think I have a responsibility as a citizen and a neighbor to do that. We all need to be diligent and look out for each other."

One of the officers walked up to the group. Caroline recognized him. "Excuse me everyone. It's time for some statements. We have four other officers and myself who will be walking each of you through what happened so we can get you all out of here and on to enjoying this beautiful day. Everyone gets to go home today. It's a good day." He looked at Caroline. "Miss Atherton, you're with me."

Caroline stepped through the crowd and smiled at the Sergeant. "Hi Sergeant. Before we get started, would it be okay if I make a quick call to my family?" She motioned toward the crowds gathering at the edge of the parking lot. "I'd hate for them to see or hear anything that way first."

"Sure. I'll be right over here." And he stepped over to the counter and helped instruct the rest of the crowd.

She fished her phone out of her purse. Unlocking the screen, she stopped. *Who do I call first? Oh dear.* She looked out the window and saw a little boy cling to his father. Looking down, she pressed the speed dial.

Two rings in, he picked up. “Hello?”

“Hey Jackson, any chance you’re still at Rick’s?” Caroline asked.

“Hey, Caroline. No, I left just a few minutes after

you. I got caught by the train, too. What's u… hey, there's quite a commotion at the corner gas station. I wonder what's up there."

"That's why I'm calling, Jackson. That's where I am." Caroline hoped her voice was steady. She did not want to frighten him.

"What!?!" Jackson shouted into the phone.

Through the window Caroline watched the traffic in the street. She saw a truck quickly turn a corner and cut off another car. Horns blared as Jackson's truck headed toward the commotion at the station.

Caroline tried to calm him. "I'm fine, Jackson. I just didn't want you to overhear anything or see anything without hearing from me first." She could see him exit his truck.

"Are you hurt, Caroline? What happened?" She could hear the rising panic in his voice.

"I'm fine, Jackson. I'm not hurt. I'm sure they won't let you in right now. Just stop and breathe. I can see you through the window." She wished waving would work, but knew he would not see her. So, she watched out the window.

"It's a madhouse out here, Caroline… I understand, officer, but my sister is in there… I'm on the phone with her right now… I don't know, sir… I will, sure. Thank you… Caroline?" Jackson was approached by one of the officers but Caroline only heard Jackson's side of the exchange.

"I'm not hurt, Jackson, I promise. I'm fine. I just have to give my statement and then I'll be good to go. There was an – incident – here in the store. A man came in with a shotgun, but no shots were fired." She said each word with emphasis. "I did step in and… kind of diffused the situation. But no shots were fired." As the adrenaline wore off, topped off by no sleep last night, she began to feel tired and weary.

The Sergeant approached her. "Miss Atherton, sorry, but the sooner we get this done, the sooner we can let life get back to normal here."

"I'll be right there," she said to the sergeant. She quickly wrapped up her call. "Jackson, I have to go. Please call Rick and let him know I'll call him just as soon as I can. I love you, Jackson."

"Love you, too, sis." Jackson ended that call and immediately placed another.

* * * * *

Things really did move along quickly. Statements and information were taken from everyone, inside and out. Within the hour everyone was finished and the lot was opening up – it would be business as usual within a few minutes.

When Caroline walked out of the store, two men

jumped up off the hood of a police cruiser just to her right. They practically ran to her side.

Jackson was the first to greet her and he scooped her up in an embrace, lifting her feet off the ground. He held her for a long time. Finally he placed her feet back on pavement and looked at her. “When you said you were in the middle of all this, everything with Mom and Dad came rushing over me. I couldn’t go through that again.”

“I know. That’s why I called you first.” She looked over at Rick with her hand out. “Sorry, Ricky.”

Rick stepped to her side and put a protective arm around her shoulders as he placed a kiss on the side of her head. “No worries.”

Caroline continued. “Stepping in wasn’t even a question. As soon as I heard the sound of the shotgun I knew I couldn’t stand by and let one of the families in that store go through what we did.” As she looked around, she recognized several of the officers from the aftermath of the tragedy that took their parents’ lives. She nodded; a faraway look in her eyes. “Today, everyone got to go home.”

She shivered. Whether from the cold or the circumstances, she couldn’t tell. Rick felt her shake. “It’s time we get her out of here, Jackson.” He looked around. His Jeep was safely parked out of the way, but media vans had moved in and surrounded it.

Rick spotted Caroline's Jeep next to pump number seven. "I'll drive her in her Jeep. You can bring me back in a little bit for mine. You make your way out of that mess," he said to Jackson as he nodded his head toward the truck surrounded by police cruisers and looky-loos. "I want to keep her way from the media circus if we can." He hesitated. "Unless you want to talk with them?"

She looked at all the cameras and what looked like a feeding frenzy waiting to happen. "I'd rather not. I may have to at some point, but I'd really rather not. If they don't have my name yet, they will soon, I'm sure. I'm not really interested in reliving both experiences with the media right now."

"Okay, then home we go." Jackson said and made his way to his truck.

As they walked to her Jeep, Caroline chuckled.

"What's so funny?" Rick asked.

Caroline looked up at Rick and grinned. "I still need gas." Caroline found the irony funny. The two chuckled as Rick held the passenger door for her. Before they made their way out of the lot, Rick put in a full tank of gas.

CHAPTER 23

It took a little finagling, but the three of them managed to get out of the mess at the gas station and made it to the house without the media in tow. Caroline was quiet in the Jeep, her thoughts on Simeon. Rick held her hand as he drove.

Once in the house, they all convened in the living room. For the next half hour, Caroline shared the experience in the gas station. The guys asked questions; she answered. Caroline was amazed at how clear some details were while others were fuzzy.

After Caroline ran through the chronicle of events she turned thoughtful. "After Mom and Dad, I knew that carrying was what I needed to do. I trained, I practiced, I took classes. I'm so thankful for what God has helped me learn and accomplish. But I never wanted to actually put it into practice. I figured it would be one of those, 'if I have it I'll never need it' kind of things."

She shuttered as she continued. "But I'll tell you, the

biggest moment of truth was when I heard the pump of the shotgun. It rang loud in my head, gave me chills all down my spine. And in a split second I had to decide if I could follow through or if I was going to let fear and insecurity control me. Only by the grace of God was I able to maintain such clarity and focus – and a steady voice."

The two men sat and listened as she shared. Their presence was exactly the support she needed.

She thought for a moment. "Talking could've gone either way. It could've made him even more angry. I'm so glad Simeon listened." A faint smile played on her face. "Hmm, he lived his name in that moment." *I'll have to share that with him when I visit him.*

The house was quiet as the three sat in thoughtful silence. Like a good patriarch offering a gentle reminder that a new day was laid out before them, the grandfather clock chimed out nine o'clock. Jackson remarked, "So much can happen in such a short time. I hope you won't think me selfish if I tell you both how glad I am to be sitting here with you right now."

Rick held Caroline's hand in his. "Too many times this year we've been reminded not to take the ones we love or the life we have for granted." Both hands enclosed hers as his thumb caressed the back of her knuckles. "It just doesn't pay to put off to tomorrow the things we can say and do today." His voice was only more than a whisper.

"I love you guys so much." Caroline took a breath. "It's also a reminder to be vigilant with our walk with God; learning his Word and being prepared to give an answer at any time. Who knew that a little history lesson could mean the difference between life and death."

* * * * *

After a time of prayer and thanksgiving for each family affected by the morning's events, God's providence and Simeon, Caroline convinced the two men to continue on with their plans for the day. Everybody had work to do, and God had given them the time to do it. She was surprised that it didn't take more convincing before the two walked out the door and Caroline was left to continue on with her own day.

Seated in her studio at her desk Caroline prepared to sort the engagement photos from Thursday's photo shoot. As she reached for her mouse, a thought made her pause. She reached behind her and pulled the holster from her belt. She slid out her handgun and looked at it. The words of Ephesians 6 came to her:

> "Finally, be strong in the Lord and in his mighty power. Put on the full armor of God so that you can take your stand against

the devil's schemes. For our struggle is not against flesh and blood, but against the rulers, against the authorities, against the powers of this dark world and against the spiritual forces of evil in the heavenly realms. Therefore put on the full armor of God, so that when the day of evil comes, you may be able to stand your ground, and after you have done everything, to stand. Stand firm, then, with the belt of truth buckled around your waist, with the breastplate of righteousness in place and with your feet fitted with the readiness that comes from the gospel of peace. In addition to all this, take up the shield of faith, with which you can extinguish all the flaming arrows of the evil one. Take the helmet of salvation and the sword of the Spirit, which is the word of God. And pray in the Spirit on all occasions with all kinds of prayers and requests. With this in mind, be alert and always keep on praying for all the saints."

Lord, thank You for the armor You've given me. Thank You that my strongest armor wasn't this, she looked at her sidearm, *but it was You. Thank You for readying my feet to stand firm against the devil's schemes and filling me with*

Your peace on this day when evil came knocking. If I had not found a peace and release from the inner battle I was fighting last week, I'm not sure I would've been prepared for this morning.

And thank you for the truth in Your word. The words were Yours, Lord, the story Yours. Two battles You've helped me fight today. One against an adversary I could not see and one I could.

Feeling a bit like a warrior, she slid the gun back into the holster and once again attached it to her belt on her hip. She turned toward her computer, opened the file of photos and began the process of sorting.

* * * * *

The alarm on her phone rang out a simple tune, drawing her attention away from the computer. *Wow, five-thirty already? How did that happen?*

Caroline had accomplished much in her day. The engagement photos were a joy to work on and really didn't take too much time to finalize. She scheduled a meeting with her clients for the next Friday to go over the next step. She returned several phone calls which bore much fruit. She had five new photo shoots sprinkled through the calendar into February. Each one accompanied by a design project as well.

The start of the new year was shaping up nicely and she would have little down time.

She worked on paperwork, her website, even got a start on year-end inventory and bookkeeping. With a contented heart she turned off her computer, packed her laptop and her camera in their bags and closed up her studio for the holiday.

Once in the house, she walked through the kitchen. *Oh, I hate to leave all this for so many days. But, I wouldn't trade our Christmas break for anything – not even finished cabinets.*

The next three nights would be spent at Rick's. The three of them had been planning their quiet, relaxing Christmas break in the country for weeks. She'd even taken a break earlier in the day to get everything she wanted packed and ready to go. Now, she loaded up all of her bags and jumped in her Jeep. With Christmas music playing loudly, she backed out and was on her way.

She spotted the house from far off. It took her a moment to realize that it was, in fact, Rick's house. The whole roof line was outlined in white lights, lighting up the sky like a beacon.

It's beautiful! Filled with a sense of joy and wonder, she pulled through the gate, up the lane and into the garage. Before she even opened the back of her Jeep to retrieve her bags Rick and Jackson were there to greet her. Each face beamed with satisfaction.

"Did you notice anything new driving in?" Rick asked with youthful exuberance.

"I think the whole town is noticing something new tonight. It lights up the whole sky. It's beautiful! How did you two fit this in your day today?"

"Oh, we called in the cavalry," said Jackson. "Small group, a couple of coaches from the center, an architect and an intern. It was a real party."

"And everyone went home in one piece – save a few cuts and scrapes." Rick added proudly. "I'm really so thankful for their help; we totally could not have pulled this off without them." He took a breath and smiled. "Surprise."

It was Caroline's turn to beam. "I love it. I can't believe you got that done just this afternoon."

Everyone took bags and boxes from the Jeep and Rick led the way into the house. "Well, we're not finished yet," said Rick over his shoulder.

Once her coat was hung up and she was out of her boots, Rick produced a large bandana. "I do have another surprise for you, but you need to play along a little." Turning her around, he slipped the bandana over her eyes as a blind fold.

Caroline giggled. "I'm a little afraid to even guess.

Just don't let me trip, please."

"Oh, I've got you. You're in good hands." Rick proceeded to lead her gingerly into the great room. He positioned her purposefully and said, "Go ahead Jackson."

The room was warm. She detected the full bodied fragrance of pine. *Mmm, what a nice smelling candle*, she thought. A barely discernable click was heard over the crackle of the fire. As the blindfold fell away, Caroline opened her eyes and gasped in disbelief. Before her stood the most beautiful Christmas tree sparkling in front of the window. Speechless, she took small steps forward as her eyes roved the creation before her taking in every aspect of the tree.

It was a beautiful, thick, freshly cut ten foot tall White Pine. The fragrance was invigorating. Its thick branches were tightly wrapped with small white lights that seemed to twinkle and wink periodically. Adorning the branches were pine cones, bright red cardinals, crystal snowflakes, cranberry clusters, medium sized red and gold glass balls, and an assortment of porcelain angels. Crowning the top of the tree rested a stunning gold filigree cut starburst.

Rick watched her. The rushed, frustrated feeling and the irritation with lights and boxes no longer mattered. The look on her face was worth any hassle he had endured. Her eyes glistened with unshed happy tears, and the sense of wonder and peace that defined her countenance made Rick so thankful he was able to pull off such an unexpected gift.

"Oh, Ricky, I don't have the words," she said as she walked around the tree.

He paused before responding; he didn't want to interrupt her moment.

"Where did all this come from?" She looked at him with wonder.

"I was walking through the woods last week and stumbled upon this beauty. Staring at it, I had an idea. Of course, you know me, my ideas have a tendency to explode into grand schemes, so Jackson helped me come up with a, what did you call it, Jackson?

"An aggressively doable plan," Jackson filled in.

Rick laughed. "Right. So, I did a little on-line shopping for the ornaments, did some quick ordering and hid everything in one of the closed up rooms. I'm kind of surprised I was able to get everything. Anyway, a friend helped me cut it down, clean it, shape it and get it in the stand. Now that was quite the education."

"And comical, too. I have pictures." Jackson snickered at the thought.

"Well, you boys have certainly been busy today. And sneaky." Caroline gave them both a sideways glance.

"Yea, I guess we've done a lot of that sneaky stuff

lately, haven't we?" Rick looked at her a little concerned.

She walked up to him, rested her hands on his chest and, smiling, said, "This was good sneaky, Ricky."

"Told you," quipped Jackson.

Caroline turned back to the tree for another look. "Well, I know where I'm spending my holiday," she said.

Rick stepped up behind her, slid his arms around her waist, and nuzzled in her ear, "with me, that's where."

She giggled and squeezed his arms tight. In the quiet of the moment a loud grumbling from her stomach sent all three into fits of laughter as they stumbled into the kitchen to start dinner.

Before she joined the men in the business of dinner prep, Caroline grabbed her bags from the mud room and made her way to her suite. "I'll be right back guys," she called over her shoulder.

Rick and Jackson looked at each other with goofy grins as she disappeared down the hall. Soft laughter emitted from each, complete with a high-five when they heard her faint exclamation.

As Caroline reached her door, she was greeted by a beautiful live evergreen wreath hanging from a large red crushed velvet bow. The wreath was lightly sprinkled with glitter, small pinecones, tiny red, green & gold Christmas balls, and five clusters of gold Christmas bells with small velvet bows.

"Oh my," she exclaimed and heard the faint sounds of laughter from the kitchen. She looked for another moment before entering her suite to drop her bags. *He's going to spoil me,* she thought, smiling.

Caroline returned to the kitchen with a smile so bright. "It's lovely, Ricky, thank you."

"You are very welcome," Rick said. "But I can't take the credit for that creation. The lady at the craft store deserves that. I told her what I wanted and she produced that gorgeous piece."

Caroline walked up close to him, clasped her hands behind her back, stood on her tippy toes and placed a gentle kiss on his cheek. "I'm still going to give you the credit," she said in a thick whisper. "Thank you."

Her feet firmly on the ground, she sauntered over to the fridge to pull out dinner fixings, her smile firmly in place.

A soft, "Wow," escaped both men. Rick looked after her in a bit of a daze, *Can I marry her now, Lord?*

Blinking his eyes, Rick looked around the room to make sure he had not actually said the words aloud. He returned to the task at hand as he reached out for the burgers. It didn't take long for the burgers to start cooking on the grill and all the condiments, side dishes and table service to be placed out on the island.

"Grilling inside. I don't think I'll ever get used to this. But I do like it." Rick held up his spatula and flipped the burgers.

CHAPTER 24

The agreed upon rules for the Christmas holiday were simple:

1. No phones
2. No electronics
3. No work
4. No outside world

They may not have been leaving town, or really home for that matter, but they were going to act as if they did. They all needed the break.

After the events of the morning, however, all three conceded to turning on the evening news, just to see who was saying what. All the stations were covering the gas station story. There were interview clips from several of the shoppers in the store, including little Charlee. Everyone had positive things to say about Caroline and how she handled the situation.

Of course, the news reporters pulled out old footage from the previous winter and played up the connection between Caroline and her parents' death in that tragedy. They showed far away footage of Caroline as she spoke with an officer and as she walked to her Jeep with Rick.

"I sure hope it all calms down soon. I don't want this kind of attention." Caroline groaned.

Rick thought for a moment. "You know, Caroline, this might not be a bad thing. You could be given the opportunity to talk with kids, women, anyone really, about the value of gun knowledge and safety, the importance of the 2nd Amendment and conceal carry. It always seems to be such a misunderstood and, all too often, feared topic. Not to mention the chance for ministry, just like with Simeon."

Caroline was uncomfortable with Rick's suggestion. "None of that is really my skill set, Ricky. What happened this morning was totally God working. Besides, I can't imagine my phone ringing off the proverbial hook with people wanting me as a speaker. I think it will all blow over after the holidays."

"You don't give yourself enough credit, Sunshine. When you're passionate about something, I don't think you realize how well you speak about it. I wouldn't be too quick to dismiss the idea. Time will tell."

*****

Long into the evening, the three sat in companionable silence in the great room. A fire continued to blaze in the fireplace, the beautiful tree sparkled in front of the window and the Trans-Siberian Orchestra piped low through the sound system. Jackson sat in an over-sized easy chair engrossed in his annual classic novel – A Christmas Carol. Caroline and Rick snuggled together on the couch.

"I can't believe all that's happened today. This morning seems like a lifetime ago," Caroline said; her voice far away.

"Hmm, it has been a full day." Rick held her a little tighter.

"I'm just amazed at how many things can happen in some days. One thing's for sure, it's a day I won't forget." She snuggled further into his arms.

"Are you really doing okay after what happened at the station? We can talk about anything you need to," he assured her.

"I know that," she smiled a confident smile at him. "And, you know, I really am. The outcome was so good, so positive. What I do want to do is to shoot though. Not because I didn't get to today, but because I want to make sure I have no hesitation, even at a paper target. I was hoping we could set things up outside tomorrow to do just that."

"Sure. I even have a spot I picked out a while ago that

I've done some shooting at. I should have everything we need."

She wrapped her arms around his and said, "This is really all I need. Nothing more."

*****

Christmas Eve dawned a new day. They ate good food, played games and just enjoyed each other's company. They took the guns out to shoot in part of the yard late in the afternoon. Rick had a couple of rifles and a .45 handgun of his own with which they all took turns. Later Jackson read more of his book. Caroline baked fudge, magic cookie bars and divinity. Rick pulled out his guitar and a stack of song books. The day was almost perfect.

Twice Rick had to address a scene on the other side of the gate at the street. The reporters had found Caroline and were loitering and pestering them from the gate. He had told them she would not talk with them and kindly asked them to leave, but they did not.

Rick finally called the police station to lodge a complaint. "If they're at my gate, they're on my property and trespassing," he told them. "If they're not at the gate then they're in the street and that's creating a hazard." Once the cruisers were by to chase them away everything was peaceful.

"I never thought I'd be glad for the gate and fence that's around the property. It kind of felt like a cage before today. I can see it now as a protective barrier; a gift for peace. It actually gives us some freedom," Rick said as he walked into the house after his second trip out.

"I don't mind it; and I'm certainly glad it's there right now." Caroline shuffled the deck of cards in her hand, looked around and asked, "Who's up for more Skip Bo?"

* * * * *

Christmas Eve night was spent much the same way as the night before. Quiet and relaxed. About nine-thirty Jackson asked, "I know we said no electronics, but would anyone mind if we put on The Nativity Story? It just doesn't feel right to miss that."

"I was afraid to say anything for fear of being chastised, but I feel the same way." Rick perked up.

"Me, three." Caroline confessed.

Once again, Rick worked on setting up the movie after he pulled it out of his collection; Jackson stoked the dwindling fire, coaxing it back to life, and Caroline popped popcorn and gathered more blankets. Sometimes life needed a little flexibility.

They all made it through the movie that time before retiring to their rooms.

* * * * *

As Caroline walked into her suite, she noticed a basket upon the center of her bed. A simple Christmas tartan ribbon was tied in a bow around the handle. Inside were six small red boxes. She looked around her room and behind her at the door. She was alone. Crossing the room, she closed her door and stood with her back against it for a moment.

He really is trying to spoil me. He's always been sweet and generous, but this is too much. She giggled and pushed off the door. *Gifts or no gifts, I am so in love with that man.* She crawled onto her bed, careful not to topple the basket, criss-crossed her legs and slowly began opening her gifts.

Caroline lifted off the lid of the first box and pulled out a wad of tissue paper. She unwrapped the little bundle to reveal an old-fashioned looking camera lapel pin. *It's perfect. Where ever did he find such a thing?*

Box number two held a tiny heart ornament with a painted, smiling sunshine. She could hear his voice in her head saying *'a little sunshine for my Sunshine.'* "Oh, this will be perfect on my table top tree in my studio next year," she whispered.

A giddy feeling overcame her as she opened the third box. "Mmm." The scent of Christmas wafted out of the box. It was one of her favorite essential oil blends and it always made her think of Christmas. Before she continued, she climbed off the bed and filled the small diffuser she kept on the dresser with water and dropped in a few drops of her new oil. She turned it on and breathed in the familiar scent. *Ah, heavenly Christmas.*

Standing before her bed, she hesitated. *I wonder if I should take this to Ricky to finish? I feel a little selfish here all by myself.* She looked around the room, pondering. *No, he wanted it to be an alone thing, otherwise he'd have given it to me when we were together. Still...*

She picked her way back onto her bed and repositioned herself. Out of the basket came box number four. Beneath the lid she found three packets of Christmas blend cocoa mix from their favorite barista and three mini candy canes. *Ah, one for each of us for Christmas day. Perfect.*

The fifth box was something unique. *A bullet? On a key chain? Hmm.* She looked a little closer and pulled at both ends. The bullet came apart to reveal a USB drive. *How clever.* "I wonder if there's anything on it."

Caroline once again shuffled off the bed and lifted her

laptop out of its bag. She waited impatiently as it booted up. With the excitement of a school girl she plugged in the flash drive and clicked on the icon to open the file. "It's a playlist. I love it," she exclaimed as she skimmed the file.

She scrutinized the song titles. "Let's see; country, jazz, classical, love songs. Ooh, all things we dance to. Oh, that man... I know what we're doing tomorrow," she said in a sing-song voice. Lost in thought, the passage of time became irrelevant as she imagined the two of them gliding around the living room floor.

Recovering from her dreamy thoughts she eventually closed the file, disconnected the drive and put away her computer. Once more she returned to the bed and her seat among the pile of goodies. There was still one box left.

Caroline reached into the basket for the remaining box. Inside nested a handful of peppermint and dark chocolate chocolates. *Oh yum. These are all mine!* She unwrapped one and savored the chocolate as it melted in her mouth.

Still sucking on her chocolate, Caroline lay back on her bed and smiled. She looked at the ceiling and began to review the thoughtful and romantic gifts Ricky had given her since their official date. *A single white rose* (the thought of the highlighted verse still made her blush), *a pair of pearl and diamond earrings, three bird feeders, the four candles of*

Advent, the wreath with clusters of Christmas bel…

She sat up straight. Quickly she hopped up off the bed and attacked her door. *One, two… five. Five clusters of Christmas bells!* Caroline saw the pattern as clear as day. *And six little gift boxes.* She turned to face her bed. She looked out the door and up the hall.

Without another thought, she hustled down the hall toward Rick's bedroom. Her pace slowed as she neared his door. A small light peeked out the bottom of the door. *Good, he's still up.* She tapped softly on the door before slowly opening it.

Shyly she looked through the door to discover Rick sitting in bed, propped up by pillows, a book in his hands. He wore black satin pajamas. *Wow, he's handsome.* She blushed and hesitated as thoughts of his words about making love rushed to her mind.

"I know it's late, Ricky, but may I come in?"

Rick closed his book and set it on the bed next to him. "Of course. There is no place in this house you aren't welcome, Sunshine. Is everything okay?" He kicked his feet over the side of the bed and rose to meet her.

Caroline stepped through the threshold, leaving the door open wide. Suddenly she felt a little nervous. She had been in Rick's bedroom before, but it felt different that night - intimate.

"Caroline?" Rick was standing before her.

She looked up at him. "The twelve days… of Christmas." She said haltingly. "Well, seven, since tomorrow is Christmas it'll be seven. You've been doing the days of Christmas."

His eyes sparkled at her words. "You caught me. I am guilty as charged. And quite proud of myself, too."

Playfully, she looked at him with dancing eyes. In mock irritation she said, "Richard Stratford, you sneaky, beguiling, clever, romantic man, you. Where ever have you found the time to do all of this?"

Rick tilted his head up and said with a distinguished air, "Oh, I'm a man of many talents." An honest and innocent smile filled his eyes. He asked. "Did you like your basket of goodies?"

"I love it." She inched closer to him, eliminating the small gap between them. Her voice soft, she said, "And I love you." Reaching a hand up around his neck, her fingers entwined his hair. She tilted her chin up to him.

He wrapped his arms around her waist, pulled her close and lowered his head for a soul quenching and tender kiss.

"I guess I can't leave you two alone at all, now, can I?" Jackson spoke from the doorway.

They slowly separated and looked at Jackson.

"Sorry," Jackson continued, "I heard voices and thought I'd investigate. I really didn't mean to interrupt."

"No worries, brother," said Rick, holding Caroline's hand.

"I left the door open. I was a good girl." Caroline smiled at her brother. Looking up at Rick, she said, "I should probably head on back to my room anyway."

"Probably." He looked at her with hungry eyes. "I'll see you in the morning." He held her hand firmly and she stopped. "And I love you, too." He kissed her hand before releasing it. She gave Jackson a quick hug and walked down the hall.

Once more the house was still; its occupants settled. One by one, the light of each room was extinguished as each quieted their thoughts and drifted off to sleep.

CHAPTER 25

Caroline woke late on Christmas morning. Instead of rushing into the day, she slowly padded across the floor to open the curtains on the French doors that lead out to her small terrace. Soft winter morning light flooded her room. She grabbed her Bible and climbed back into bed where she arranged some pillows and leaned against the headboard, her covers bunched up around her like a fluffy cloud.

With her Bible at her side, she hugged her knees and looked out at the beautiful, picture-perfect scene before her. *I don't know why I have the privilege of being here among all this beauty, Lord, but I thank You so much.*

There was a quiet knock at the door. "Who is it?" she called.

"Just your friendly neighborhood Christmas Elf."

She giggled. "Come on in, Jackson."

Jackson opened the door and strode over to her bed. He was wearing his usual bedtime attire – sweat pants and a t-shirt. He grabbed a handful of pillows on his way over and tossed them against the footboard. He sat opposite her and said, "Merry Christmas, sis."

"Merry Christmas, big brother. Have you been up long?"

"No, the house is still quiet. Looks like we all had the same idea this morning." He was silent for a moment. "I've got a silly question that kind of makes me feel like I'm five."

Caroline chuckled, "It's Christmas, it's okay to feel five. What's your question?"

"Well," he hesitated, "have you by any chance thought about Christmas Tree Bread?" He looked at her with a hope-filled expression; just the kind of look a five year old would give.

Christmas Tree Bread had been a staple of Christmas morning their whole lives. Their mom always had two cookie sheets baked and ready to devour for breakfast every year. Caroline had thought long about how to carry on that particular tradition. She was glad he had thought of it, too.

With her own mix of grown up and five year old she said, "It's just not Christmas or <u>our</u> family without it. Obviously, it won't be ready for breakfast. I could never figure out how Mom made that happen. But, it <u>is</u> Christmas, and <u>we</u> are family. I'd already planned on making it."

His smile filled his face. "You're awesome, Caroline."

She feigned embarrassment. "Awe, shucks."

Jackson's expression changed as he looked around the room. His face set with a confident look, he gave his head a quick, decisive nod and said, "You know, I think I'm going to like it here when I move in."

Caroline frowned in confusion. "I didn't realize you were talking about moving out of the house."

"Oh, I'm not. But once you and Rick get married you won't be needing this suite any longer for your own private use. I'll get it. Give you love birds some privacy on the other side of the house." Jackson wiggled his eyebrows at her.

She threw a pillow at him. "Jackson Atherton! Don't tease me."

"Well, isn't that the ultimate goal of this courtship?" he asked innocently.

"Well, yes, I… suppose it is" she looked down shyly, "but we haven't really talked about that, specifically. And I, I don't want to presume too much too soon."

"Oh, please. I could feel the heat from that kiss last night from across the room. And those bedroom eyes? Oh, yea! I'll be moving my stuff down this hall pre-tty soon."

"Jackson!"

"What? I'm just tellin' it like I see it." He softened his tone, and his expression, "and I'm glad, little sister. I can't tell you how glad."

She took a breath. "That means a lot, Jackson, thank you."

"Ah, so this is where the party is." Rick leaned in through the doorway. "Is there room for one more?" He still wore his satin PJs, now also clad in a charcoal gray fleece robe.

"Absolutely, brother, come on in. Besides, it is your house."

"No, not this suite. This is Caroline's. I don't come in here." He looked at her with a guilty grin, "Well, not usually."

Quickly, Caroline looked at Jackson and explained his look. "He left a basket of goodies on the bed for me. That's all." She took a breath and smiled. "Actually, that's why I was down the hall last night. I wanted to thank him."

"And I'm sure he appreciated your… appreciation." Jackson snickered at his own cleverness.

Rick and Caroline both groaned while Rick pulled a chair up next to the bed. Leaning onto the bed he gave Caroline a kiss on the cheek. "Merry Christmas, Sunshine."

Both hands on his face, she smiled. "Merry Christmas, Ricky."

Rick settled into his chair, kicked his feet up on the bed and asked, "So, what's the plan?"

Jackson and Caroline just shrugged.

"What, didn't this clever meeting of the minds come up with anything before I got here?" Rick asked.

"Yes, but not about today." Jackson shot Caroline a mischievous look.

Caroline shot back with a warning look.

Ignoring his sister Jackson continued with all the joy of Christmas his voice could conjure. "Well, except Caroline's going to make Christmas Tree Bread."

"Oh, yeah? Awesome!" With a youthful glow of delight he looked at Caroline. "Thanks, Sunshine." He looked at Jackson. "Well, since it won't be for breakfast, let's go make some bacon and eggs. I'm hungry."

The two jumped up and headed for the kitchen.

"I'll join you two in a few," Caroline called after them. She closed her door and set about preparing for the day.

*****

While the bread dough was rising, they all decided to take a snow walk in the woods. No reporters or looky-loos hovered about so they were free to roam around and enjoy themselves and the property. With the bare winter trees, they did not need to concern themselves with a trail, they could just wander and explore to their hearts content.

Rick and Caroline held hands. Jackson and Rick engaged in a fierce snowball battle. And Caroline took pictures. She even handed her camera off to Jackson for a few shots of her and Rick. Her camera was not a good 'selfie' camera. Setting the camera aside, they all fell into the snow and indulged in a favorite childhood activity – snow angels. They even rolled up a snowman in the front yard; his job was to wave at passers-by.

As noses turned numb, they all made for the house for some special Christmas hot cocoa as they thawed out before the fire. Plus the Christmas Tree Bread would need to be shaped before much longer.

Caroline pulled out the dough and separated it into two large sections. As she pulled the sections apart to roll into balls to form the Christmas trees, Rick joined her in the kitchen.

"Looks like we're running low on firewood. I thought I'd stacked enough, but we've used more than I realized. Jackson and I are going to go out and do some real-man work. We're going to go cut firewood in the woods." He flexed a muscle man pose for her at which she promptly giggled. "Anyway, that will give you the house to yourself for a little while. You good?"

"Sounds good to me. Once I'm finished and I clean up here, I'm sure I can find some way to entertain myself. Be safe."

"We will. Love you." And he leaned over the counter and gave her a quick kiss – on the lips. Rick stepped back, headed toward the garage, and did an about-face twirl in the kitchen. "Wow, I'm sorry." He looked at her, his eyes wide with concern. "That just felt so… natural." *Like what married people do.*

Caroline lowered her eyes with a shy smile. "Yes, it did." *And I liked it.*

"I'll… try to do better." Conflicted, Rick haltingly turned and joined Jackson in the garage.

Caroline was just as conflicted. *O, Lord, help us to honor you in this time. Time. How much time, Lord?* She watched the two men out the kitchen window as they disappeared into the woods; each pushed a wheel barrow containing an axe and a saw. *For as far as we've come in such a short time, we still have so many things to learn and discuss.*

She continued rolling the dough into balls as she thought and prayed. *But what's the right amount of time for us? Life is so fragile and our time together so short; I don't want to be constantly waiting through any more of it. And yet, I know there is much waiting in life and I don't want to rush in <u>my</u> timing, Lord, I want so much to be in Yours. Show us Your path, Lord.*

Her mind was focused on prayer as she finished shaping her trees. Once all the dough balls had been placed, she covered the two pans with damp cloths and set them on the counter to rise. A timer was set so she wouldn't forget them.

* * * * *

With the house all to herself, and a more contented and peaceful spirit after her prayer time, Caroline skipped to her room where she retrieved the flash drive Rick gave her filled with music. Plugging it into the sound system, she set the volume up loud and looked around the formal living room. The room still remained completely empty. Once in a while, when they had the time, she and Rick used it as a dance floor. And that is exactly what she intended to do with her alone time.

Since she didn't have a dance partner, she decided on a little country line dancing. Music cued, she slid and turned and cha-cha-ed all around the room.

Rick and Jackson brought a few wheelbarrows full of wood to the large woodbox by the garage door. Each time they heard the music loudly from within.

Jackson tried several times to sneak a peak through one of the windows.

"What is she doing in there?" Rick asked as he stacked wood.

"I don't know," said Jackson as he jumped off the wood box. "I can't see her."

Rick threw another log onto the stack. "Hmm, she must be in the living room. That sounds like the music I gave her in one of her gifts." He smiled as the thought of her dancing around his home danced through his mind.

Jackson watched Rick's face out of the corner of his eye as he threw the last of the logs in the box. "You want to go join her."

Rick picked up the tools from the ground and walked back toward the woods. "I'll get there. Let's get this finished. One more full load oughta do it."

Finally, with an abundance of wood stacked they were satisfied that it would last for several days – even with how much they expected to use it. Stepping into the house, they shed their gear and followed the music. Caroline was mid-way through the Cowboy Cha Cha when they discovered her. Leaned against opposite sides of the door jam, they watched her.

I'll never put a stick of furniture in here if this is what it'll be used for. Man, she looks good. Rick watched her turn, admiring the fluidity of her movement, aching to hold her and glide across the floor with her.

Not able to contain his admiration, Rick let out a cat call; grinning from ear to ear.

Caroline added an extra turn and looked up. "Uh oh, you caught me." She was breathless as the song ended. After only a brief pause another began. "Electric Slide. Come on and join me boys!"

Jackson jumped in. "Oh yea."

Rick sauntered in, eagerly and reluctantly. "Only if I get a jitter bug next."

Caroline grinned. "You're on!"

* * * * *

The three danced away the rest of the afternoon. A little swing, a little hip hop, a little waltz. Mid-way through Caroline put the bread in the oven to bake. Then they resumed their dancing. At the sound of the timer, they took another break to ice and eat the bread.

Just like all the years past, they stood in the kitchen and savored the Christmas treat.

Rick reminisced. "I remember that first Christmas I spent with you guys. I stumbled into the kitchen to see everyone standing around a pan of bread in your pajamas. I thought you all were a little crazy."

Caroline laughed. "We must've looked like vultures."

"I have a confession," said Jackson. "That first year, I hoped you'd keep sleeping so I wouldn't have to share. I was a little disappointed when you appeared while we were eating."

Rick gave Jackson a shove. "Gee, thanks brother!"

Jackson reclaimed his spot at the island. "Yea, I know, you're shocked. Here you thought all this time I was so virtuous and generous. Now you know the truth."

Caroline watched the two men. "Well, I for one am glad we have this tradition." She held up a dough ball that dripped with creamy white icing. "To tradition."

Rick and Jackson each held up a dough ball. They mushed their hands together in a sticky mess and said in unison, "Tradition."

****

For the first time in hours, the house was quiet as they all relaxed in the great room – Jackson in the overstuffed easy chair, Caroline on the couch and Rick on his back on the floor.

Rick lay there mesmerized by the twinkling lights of the Christmas tree, deep in thought, when he suddenly realized, *Today is Christmas. It's today.*

CHAPTER 26

Rick bolted upright and looked at the others. "Hey guys, did we forget that it's Christmas?"

Confused, Jackson asked, "What do you mean?"

Rick pointed at the tree. Sometime throughout the night before, each had sneaked out to place their gifts below or around the tree.

Caroline piped up, "Oh, presents! Of course."

Jackson uncrossed his feet and leaned forward. "I guess it just goes to show you that when you're surrounded by such great fellowship, material things can't compare." He rested his elbows on his knees. "Well, Rick, you're the Master of the House. Would you like to do the honors?"

"Whoa, Master of the House. I like that. And yes, I will do the honors." He crawled over to the tree and looked at the gifts. "I think we'll do it this way this year. Ladies first. Caroline, why don't you hand out your gifts."

"Ohh, goodie." She jumped up and reached under the tree for her gifts. One big box and one small box. She looked at her hands. *Which one first?* She looked from Rick to Jackson. *Not married yet.* She walked across the floor and handed the big box over to Jackson.

It wasn't often Caroline found her brother speechless. When he lifted off the top to the box, he looked inside and stared. His eyes filled with tears. Inside the box rested the Atherton family Bible and their parents' wedding rings. All he managed to choke out was the word, "Where?"

Tears slid down her cheeks as she answered softly, "I don't know how they ended up together, but I was cleaning out a closet one day and there they were. It's more like a gift from God, than me. Merry Christmas, Jackson." Up on her knees at his side, she hugged him tightly.

After she dried her tears, Caroline turned and shuffled on her knees over to Rick. She handed him the small box.

Rick unwrapped his gift and opened the box. He was taken back by the perfect, well, timing of her gift as he lifted out an antiqued pocket watch with a Celtic style cross on the cover. Turning it over he discovered an engraving.

He read it aloud, "Eccl. 3:1 'There is a time for everything; and a season for every activity under heaven.'" He looked at her. "It's more perfect than you know, Caroline. Thank you."

Her eyes held a secret as she said, "Open it."

He cocked his head curiously and pressed the button.

Tucked inside the cover was a photo of the two of them, on the yacht, dancing. "How did you get this? I haven't even seen any of the photos yet."

She just smiled brightly. "I guess it was my turn to be sneaky. Merry Christmas, Ricky."

Rick stared at her, wanting to kiss her. He leaned forward and brushed his lips gently against her cheek. "Thank you, Sunshine." He sat back and took another long look at the photo.

He closed the watch and looked over at Jackson. "Your turn, brother."

Jackson had to work a little harder to retrieve his gifts. He pulled one large square box from behind the left side of the tree and slid it toward Caroline.

"Oh my, that's quite a box," she said. Jackson was a meticulous wrapper so it took her some time to tear the paper and cut the tape, but she finally got to the inside. She employed a little help from her brother, and it took both of them to convince the box to give up its prize. Unwrapping the bubble wrap, Caroline gasped; a well-spring of tears flowed unchecked as she stared - at her family.

It was the last family photo taken of all five of them, last Christmas out on the grounds of Rick's home. Caroline had set up her tripod and spent about an hour posing the five of them for family pictures. They'd laughed so hard – it felt more like a photo session with toddlers than grown-ups. Little did they know that it would be the last time they would take a photo together.

Caroline could barely focus through her tears. In her hands she held one of her prints, enlarged, double matted, and stunningly framed in a beautiful 27" x 40" cherry wood frame with intricate scroll work.

Through her tears she said, "I haven't been able to look through last year's photos. I've tried and I just haven't been able to. I don't know how you did this, Jackson, and I don't care. Thank you so much."

It was Jackson's turn to hug his sister long and tight. "Merry Christmas, sis. I love you."

Jackson slid the frame to lean safely against a wall. Turning back to the tree, he pulled out an even bigger square box from along the right side of the tree and slid it over to Rick.

"Good heavens, Jackson. What did you do?" Like a little kid, Rick tore into his gift. The paper slipped off the box revealing a drawing and description of its contents. It was a gorgeous mahogany drafting table. Quickly, Rick discarded the remaining paper.

Rick's last personal table from his townhouse had gone to the office when he hired Tom. Consequently, when he worked from home, he used a simple folding table. It was less than ideal, but he couldn't justify spending the money for a new one. He rarely worked from home, so it seemed an unnecessary extravagance.

"Oh, wow, Jackson, this is amazing. I can't believe you did this. How did you know which one to get?" Rick gave Jackson a fond embrace.

"I spoke with Marjory and Tom. They were great. Took all the guess work out of it. Merry Christmas, brother."

"Wow. Thank you. I know just the place for it, too." Rick flashed Jackson a smile filled with hidden meaning. "And I can't wait to put it together, later."

Eventually, Rick slid the box off to the side and leaned it against the wall.

As Rick returned to his seat, Jackson said to him, "Okay, your turn."

Rick took a breath. He walked to the tree and pulled out a cylindrical shaped gift. Without hesitation he handed it over to Jackson.

"Hmm, I wonder where he gets his wrapping containers from?" Jackson quipped as he took the gift. For as meticulous as he was about wrapping a gift, he did not hold to the same standard for unwrapping. He tore into the paper and quickly popped off the top of the cylinder. As he looked inside, he discovered that it was not paper rolled up in there.

"Yea, brother! This is awesome!" Jackson called out

as he unraveled the personalized jersey of his favorite hockey player. An envelope fell out of the folds of the jersey. Opening it he discovered a pair of tickets to each of six home games. "Hockey night, you and me!" They high-fived and fist bumped in excitement.

"Merry Christmas, brother," said Rick.

Rick and Caroline enjoyed Jackson's excitement as he slipped into his new jersey and checked the dates on the tickets.

"Thanks, brother," Jackson said. "We're gonna have some fun this winter." He set the tickets aside after a moment, a grin firmly established upon his face. "Okay," he said, "I'm done. I won't hog the night."

Rick rubbed his hands together and let out a slow breath. *I sure hope this works.* It was time for Caroline's gift. She sat up on the edge of the couch and watched as he walked her way, no gift in his hand. He knelt down before her.

"As you discovered last night, I started my own little version of the days of Christmas. With today being day seven I was having trouble coming up with a 'seventh day of Christmas.' I prayed about it and searched the internet about it, but I just wasn't satisfied with what I was finding. And then it hit me. I already had the perfect thing. But it's not really a thing, so you have to listen for this one. Are you ready?"

Caroline was a little confused. She looked at Jackson, but he didn't look confused or concerned. She looked back at Rick. "Okay, I guess so."

Rick looked into Caroline's eyes, held her hands in his and said, "I love you, will you marry me?"

Caroline now looked more confused. *Marry me? Did he just ask me to marry him? Now, Lord? Could You really mean now is okay?*

Rick looked at Jackson. "I did count right, didn't I?"

Jackson grinned and nodded.

Out of his pocket Rick pulled a little velvet-covered box. "Perhaps this will help, Sunshine." He opened the box to reveal the most exquisite ring Caroline had ever seen. It took her breath away. It was the sunshine, in diamonds, set in white gold.

"Will you be my forever bride, Sunshine?" Rick looked at her with love and sincerity. "That was seven, too, in case you wondered."

Again she thought, *He asked me to marry him? Now? So soon. Too soon? I've known him fourteen years, this is not soon. I want more than anything to marry him.* Her mind raced and jumped in a jumble as she tried to process her feelings. *I don't feel nervous... or anxious... or uncertain... or doubtful,* she thought. *So what do I feel?*

Filled with confidence and a certainty that excited her all the way down to her toes, Caroline knew that all she felt was – certain. *He's waiting, Caroline! Tell him, tell him now!*

"Yes. Yes, I'll marry you, Ricky."

As he took her hand in his, she quickly grabbed it back. "Wait! Are you sure? We only just started this." Suddenly she was concerned.

"Am I sure?" Rick asked with a laugh. "Sunshine, I told you the night of our date that I wanted to be your one lover for life and that I was completely committed to you and this path we were on. Yes, I'm sure. I've never been more sure of anything in my life."

He placed his hands on either side of her knees. "We know all too well how precious life is. I'm not content to just sit around and wait, I want to live my life with you, starting as soon as possible. But it's not just about what I want. I also told you I've committed this, all of this, to the Lord and I want to do this in His timing."

Rick sat back on his feet, his hands drifted down to her ankles. He looked over at Jackson before he continued. "After a few more guy talks with Jackson, a lot of prayer and seeking His word, I feel completely confident that we are in His timing."

As his passion rose, so did his hands, back to her knees, his palms up. "And, as if I needed more confirmation, your gift was it. Without a doubt I already knew. This <u>is</u> our time Caroline. Right now."

She could feel his passion bubble up inside her. Slowly, she placed her hand back in his where he tenderly placed the ring on her finger. It fit perfectly. Rising on his knees, barely an inch from her face, he said, "Jackson, I'm going to kiss your sister again."

"Okay, I'll close my eyes," Jackson said as he leaned forward, resting his elbows on his knees, an easy smile about his lips.

Her face in his hands; her hands on his chest, he pulled her into a tender and passionate kiss. If a kiss could be filled with promise, it was that kind of kiss.

*****

Rick reluctantly pulled back as the warning bells began to sound. He looked at her once more hungrily. "Oh, I need to watch that. You, my darling, are intoxicating."

She held onto his hand greedily and sighed. "Wow!"

As the warning bells in his head faded, Rick remembered one last thing. His eyes danced with a happy secret. "I have something else for you. And now it's so much more appropriate to give to you." He made his way to the tree where, tucked deep in the back was one more cylindrical shape.

"You've already given me more than enough, Ricky," Caroline said as she received the gift, her eyes still sparkling.

"Yea, well, I guess I was on a roll," Rick said. "Go ahead – open it." His eyes shone with expectation.

She unwrapped the drafting tube and pulled the cap off the end. As she looked inside, she said with a curious tone, "It really is paper." She pulled out the roll of paper and began to spread it out on the floor. "It's blueprints." *What has he done now?*

Jackson joined Rick and Caroline on the floor. Each of the guys held down the corners so she could get a full look at what was on the paper. She looked, and read, and tried to make sense of it. She read the labels aloud, "make up/bathroom; back drops/props, studio, drafting…"

She noticed the words 'main house', 'bird sanctuary' and 'prayer corner' and the blueprint suddenly sprang to life. "It's a new studio and office!" she exclaimed. "Here! For you and me?"

"I knew she was smart." Rick said to Jackson.

Caroline tumbled over her words. "When? How? You… oh my goodness, Ricky, this is amazing!"

"It's a pretty good representation of what I've got floating around in my mind, but, of course, I need to hash it all out with you before the plans are finalized. It's far more yours than mine. I have my office. But you need to have your own sanctuary and place to work, here, at home, that meets all your needs. And when I get to work from home I'll have a spot right there with you. I'm hoping to break ground as soon as spring will allow."

"Home," Caroline said sounding a bit dreamy. "This will officially be my home, too". *I like the sound of that so much.* Her smile faded as she remembered the conversation she'd had with Jackson earlier in the morning. Caroline looked at her brother accusingly. "You knew – all of this." It was not a question.

He shrugged. "Well, yes. But, remember, good sneaky. This was good sneaky."

"Right. Good sneaky." She looked at Rick. "No more good sneaky for a while, please."

"Alright, Sunshine." He looked sideways at Jackson. "Her birthday's not 'til summer; do you think that's long enough?"

Caroline groaned and playfully pushed each of them over. Laughter filled the house as they spent the rest of the night talking about future plans.

Here's a little sneak peek at what I'm working on for

"Discovering Days of Summer"
Book 2 of the "Days of..." Series

She leaned against the window frame and looked out into the darkness searching for the faint vision of the gently falling snow under the soft glow of the lights shining off the back of the house. Although her view was obstructed by the bright lights from within, she could just make out the sight of snowflakes. Lost in her thoughtful reverie she didn't notice him walk up behind her.

"A penny for your thoughts," he whispered in her ear as he slid his hands around her waist and rested his head against hers. He looked at her reflection in the window and smiled.

She closed her eyes, sighed and drank in the feel of his touch. Opening her eyes she smiled at his reflection in the window. "First, a nickel for a kiss."

He turned his head to kiss her on the temple. "And I won't charge you; I'll just tell you that I love you."

She shifted in his arms, leaning her back against the window frame, looking him full in the face. Smiling, she rested her hands on his forearms. "And I love you." A faraway look clouded her eyes. "I was just thinking I'll miss having Mom and Dad here tonight. They would've enjoyed our announcement."

A sad smile darkened his features. "I've thought the same thing. Kind of puts a little cloud over things a bit, doesn't it? But, I choose to believe they'd be on board with this."

They stood in reflective silence for a few moments, once again gazing out the window at the falling snow, his arm around her shoulder. Jazz music filtered through the home in the background, mixed with the laughter and chatter of friends.

It was New Year's Eve and Caroline, Rick and Jackson were hosting an intimate gathering for their singles small group and a handful of other friends. What their friends did not know was that Caroline and Rick planned to share some special news. What Jackson did not know was that his world was about to knocked off-kilter.

Look for *Book 2* to release in the Spring of 2017.

Feel free to copy this page and make your own bookmark.

Love is:
Patient
Kind
Joyful
Humble
Encouraging
Polite
Selfless
Calm/Even
Tempered
Forgiving
Pure
Protective

Article [II] (Amendment 2) of the Constitution of the United States

"A well regulated Militia, being necessary to the security of a free State, the right of the people to keep and bear Arms, shall not be infringed."

Knowledge is Power! We are much stronger when we are educated. This is here simply to educate and inform. If you are interested in learning more about firearms and firearm safety, contact a shooting range in your area or your local Conservation Department to start. You will readily find someone who can point you in the right direction and offer help.

Always exercise wisdom and caution, and be diligent to learn the specific laws of your state, county, and city.

The Well-Armed Woman is another resource to educate and guide you on your own journey of firearm safety and training. See the vast array of resources available on their website.

https://thewellarmedwoman.com/

ABOUT THE AUTHOR

Born and raised in southern California, Sharon knew from the time she was a teenager that California was not where she belonged. Inspired by the nostalgia of small-town living depicted in a movie, she relocated when she was 21 to the Mid-West in hopes of finding her "Ben" and a quiet, simple life. Four years later she did, indeed, meet her "Ben" and was married a year later.

Sharon now resides on the outskirts of the Kansas City Metropolitan area with her husband and two sons. Although 'quiet' might not be the word to describe her life, she would not trade her time home with her kids, homeschooling, for anything. Her time homeschooling her boys has stretched her, strengthened her, encouraged her, and enriched her.

Sharon would say that her life has been characterized by stepping out in faith. From relocating half-way across the country on her own to walking cluelessly into the worlds of theatre and archery on her sons' behalf, she has relied heavily on her Heavenly Father's guidance and instruction. Through the ups and downs, joys and challenges of life, her overriding purpose and passion lie in the Lord and His word. Embarking on this journey of writing is a new step out in faith as she desires to share her deep love for the Lord and encourage others to live their life deeply rooted in a relationship with Him, and live it boldly.

Stay connected to Sharon and her upcoming book releases at her website and her facebook page. If you are interested in having Sharon share at your group or event, please feel free to contact her at one of the following:

sharondtweet@gmail.com.

www.sharondtweet.wordpress.com

www.facebook.com/SharonDTweetAuthor/

Made in the USA
Monee, IL
27 October 2023

45335955R00149